A Novel

THE GRAY BROTHERS: THE BEGINNING

JOHANNA DELACRUZ

DISCLAIMER

All material is of mature content and theme. I advise reader discretion.

I dedicate this book to a set of brothers I grew up with, who I hold near and dear to my heart.

CHAPTER 1

THE GRAYS

I was looking for something in my room, like my keys, when Mom opened the door. "Patty, I need you to take something over to Lucille."

I stood up and looked at her. "Not the romance novels," I groaned.

"She wants to read the recent one I finished," she spoke in a casual tone. I knew that tone. She didn't use it for the heck of it; There was always a hidden meaning behind it.

"Mom, I hate when you send me over there," I grumbled.

"Oh, come on, you enjoy seeing Lucille," she reminded me.

"Yeah, Lucille, but every time I go over there, I have to deal with the boys," I groaned.

"What's wrong with the boys? They're charming and polite, youthful men."

If she only knew the truth about the Gray boys. See, my mom was a little naïve with the Gray boys; that's because they pulled the wool over her eyes. Hey Mrs. George, they would greet her. How you, Mrs. George? You get the point.

It was a wholly unique thing for me. I was like a little sister to them since my older brother was friends with them. Well, that's what they have told me except meaner, but so was my brother. Never mind, I'm getting off track.

Lucille and Grayson have lived across the street, kitty-corner from us, for as long as I can remember. They had three boys. Nathaniel Mark seven years older than I and has a temper. Jonas Allen, two years younger than Nathaniel, and always had his head in a book. Finally, there was Cayson David, two years younger than Jonas, and the baby. He hung out with my brother the most.

They were all hell raisers and loved to give me a hard time. They said it was because they saw me as the sister they never had. But do brothers blow up your Barbie dolls or chase stray cats with remote control cars? No, well, at least mine doesn't. Dad would kill him if he did.

I looked at my mom, and she grinned. I rolled my eyes, and she laughed while handing me a bag with books. I was so not getting out of this one. I snatched the bag from her hands and walked out of my room.

It was a conspiracy between her and Lucille, but I'll get to that later.

Carrying the bag of books in hand, I walked across the street. I made sure I checked for cars since they drive like nuts down this street. I walked up the driveway to hear someone cursing and throwing stuff around. Great, Nate was home.

I made my way to the front door, trying to avoid him. Ever since I broke his toy model as a kid, he never let me forget it. It was an accident. I thought you could play with it. Mom offered to buy him another one.

Before even making it to the front door, I heard someone bellow, "Hey, it's Peppermint, Patty!" I winced at that nickname. I turned to see Jonas grinning at Nate and me looking over the hood of the car. Ugh, thanks, Mom.

Nate smirked, and I shot him a glare. I pulled them both a glare.

"Looks like someone's pissed," I heard another voice say. Cayson, where the hell did he come from since I didn't see him? He handed Nate a tool.

"What else is new?" Nate remarked as he went back to working on his car.

I sighed, walking up to the door, and knocked. Lucille answered it. "Patty! What a pleasant surprise? Come in," she waved me in, and I walked by her. She looked at the boys. "You boys, be nice."

"We're always nice, ma," Jonas responded.

"Uh, huh? Oh, and Nate?"

He looked up, irritated. "Yeah?"

"I need your help here."

"Has Jonas help you," he answered in an annoyed tone.

"Nathaniel Mark, I'm sure I asked you to help me." She shot him a look.

"Whatever," he mumbled as he tossed a wrench to the side and went into the garage.

She went back into the house, letting the screen door close behind her. I was standing in the kitchen after setting the books down on the table. I watched her walked over to a chair, pick it up, and carry it over to a light fixture. What is she doing?

"Hit the lights, would you?" she asked me.

I flipped the switch. Lucille took down the light globe, then whacked a utensil against the bulbs, breaking them. Then Lucille replaced the light cover and got down. I watched her put the chair back and clean up the glass.

"That should do it," she remarked as she brushed her hands together.

"Did you break those bulbs on purpose?" I asked, confused.

"Who? Why would little old me do that? Why nonsense? And you saw nothing," she answered as she gave me a look, and I raised my brows.

A few minutes later, Nate stomped into the house. "Okay, what do you need?"

"There is something wrong with the kitchen light. I went to turn it on, and it wasn't coming on," Lucille said.

He grabbed a stepladder and placed it under the light fixture, taking off the globe. Then his expression changed. "How the hell did the bulbs break?"

"Got me. Such a mystery," Lucille shrugged. Uh-huh, sure, because your mom broke them you doof.

"Hang on, I'll go get some needle-nose pliers," he told her, stepping down.

"Good, Patty help you," she commented, shoving me at him. I lost my footing and fell with him catching me. I looked up into his steel-grey eyes, and he looked down into my ocean blue eyes. He helped me to my feet.

"Sorry," I gulped.

"No worries. Come on." Nate turned and walked away. I turned to look at Lucille, and she waved at me to follow him. I turned and pursued him into the basement.

Why did this feel like this was a setup?

CHAPTER 2

NATHANIEL GRAY AKA NATE

I followed Nate downstairs into the basement. I watched as he moved his hair out of his face as he looked for a pair of pliers. Damn, he was hot. Focus Patty. He is not sexy. He is a thorn in your side. Plus, he is seven years older than me.

He pulled out a toolbox and opened it, rummaging through the contents. "Sometimes, my ma does these things on purpose," he mumbled.

"Huh?" I looked at him.

"My ma, she does this shit on purpose," he said, staring at me. He was making me uncomfortable. When we were kids, it was different. He would tease me, but now there was like some weird tension between us, which was never there before.

Oh, I know she does these things on purpose. I've seen it firsthand.

"Found it," he said, holding up a pair of needle-nose pliers.

"Huh?" I asked, breaking from my thoughts.

He shoved the pliers in my face, "Pliers."

I gave him a look as I furrowed my brows. He walked up the stairs, and I followed behind him. He climbed onto the stepladder and started getting the base of the bulbs out of the socket. Lucille flipped the switch, causing a pop sound and Nate to fall off the ladder. She flipped it down and acted.

I looked at her as she whistled. This woman was nuts.

"Go see how he's doing?" She said, pushing me towards him.

"Shouldn't you see how he's doing considering he's your son?" I questioned her.

"I have to check on Jonas and Cayson. Bye," she said, leaving the kitchen. I opened my mouth, trying to stop her, and she was already through the door leading into the garage. What is wrong with this woman? She tried to electrocute her son.

I walked over to Nate and helped him up. "Are you okay?"

He sat up and looked at me. "Did you flip that switch?"

"What? No," I defended myself.

He stood up and yanked his arm away from me. "Yeah, right," he scoffed.

"But I didn't," I protested, but he waved me off. I won't stand by and get blamed for something his mother did. I opened the screen door of the garage and walked by the three of them.

"Patty, where are you going, hun?" Lucille asked me.

"Home," I answered, not bothering to turn around. Stupid Nate, simple light switch.

I watched to make sure no cars were coming before I ran across the street. I don't know why things changed between the Gray boys and me. It was like the dynamics changed.

I walked into the house, past Mom. I went to my bedroom in the back of the house next to the bathroom and kitchen. I grabbed my car keys and purse, leaving.

I got into the car and drove over to Liz's house. I needed to vent to someone. Who is the best person to vent to, but my best friend?

"You were at their house?" She asked. "And you didn't call me?"

"My mom sent me over with a bag of romance novels for Lucille. It's not like I wanted to be there on purpose," I said.

"Why not? I would go there on purpose. Those boys are freaking hot," she smirked as she plopped down on her bed next to me.

"And they're also a pain in the ass. Do you know Nate accused me of trying to electrocute him?" I stood up and paced back and forth.

"Well, did you?" She questioned me.

I stopped and looked at her. "No, Lucille flipped the damn switch."

"Wait, why did his mother try to electrocute her son?" She asked me, confused.

"Got me. Why does Lucille do half the things she does? She does." I shrugged as I sat down on the bed in a huff.

"Patty, you have liked Nate your entire life. It's your chance." She smiled at me.

"Liz, Nate is twenty-four and usually has a girlfriend. Plus, I like Brian Holloway," I sighed.

Brian Holloway was my dream guy. He was a senior like us and every girl's fantasy, plus he was cute. Now I needed the nerve to talk to him.

"Forget Brian Holloway. He is such a douche."

"He is not!" I exclaimed.

"Trust me; he is," she said to me.

"That's a persona," I said, blowing off her comment.

"Don't say I didn't warn you. Patty, I still think you should go after one of the Gray boys. They're your neighbors, they're funny, and they're freaking hot."

"You're no help," I groaned.

"I'm a girl with raging hormones, so sue me," she smirked, and I couldn't help but laugh. At least she was honest.

CHAPTER 3

JONAS GRAY

I left Liz's place and made my way to the store. Mom asked me to pick her up an item, so I looked for my keys and interrupted to take books to Lucille.

I walked into the store and ended up in the feminine hygiene product aisle. I don't even know why I got sent to pick up pads since Mom would be grocery shopping.

I looked at all the different pads and finally found her brand. I picked up a pack and walked to the register. I bumped into none other than Brian Holloway, dropping the package of pads on the floor. He was with a girl and looked at me. I wanted to crawl in a hole and die right now.

"Patty, there you are," someone announced.

My eyes widened as Jonas Gray walked up. He leaned down and picked up the package off the floor. "Thanks for helping me pick these out for my ma. It's crazy to think she needed to send me to the store for them."

I didn't know what to say. Jonas turned and looked at Brian. "Jonas Gray, Patty's neighbor, and honorary big brother," he introduced himself. Jonas held out his hand.

"Brian Holloway, this is Tricia Holcomb, my girlfriend." Those words ripped through my heart, shredding it into a million pieces. Now I wanted to crawl into a hole and die.

Jonas glanced at me then looked at Brian and smiled. "That's super, but we should get going. Nate is waiting for Patty."

Brian gave him a look. "Isn't he like thirty or something?"

"He's twenty-four but could pass for eighteen. Gets impatient if you know what I mean?" Jonas responded, winking and clicking his teeth. Will someone shoot me and put me out of my misery?

He took my arm and led me away. He leaned over and whispered, "Play along. He's still watching."

"But I am not with your brother," I whispered to him.

"Yeah, but he doesn't know that," he whispered back to me. The cashier scanned the pads and looked at Jonas. "What? Sometimes you need those super-absorbent pads on those big days."

I placed my hand on my face. Did Jonas recite a commercial about pads?

She totals the amount, and he handed her some cash paying for the pads. She gave him the change, which he took along with the pads. He started walking away, and I chased after him.

He was already halfway out into the parking lot as I ran after him. His lean six foot one frame towered over me. His dark blonde locks were short and spiky, with his green eyes offsetting them.

Out of the brothers, Jonas had a quirky sense of humor. He was always in a pleasant mood. I don't think I ever saw him in a foul mood.

I finally caught up with him as he turned and tossed the bag to me. I caught it.

"Thanks," I mentioned to him.

"Don't worry about it, Peppermint Patty," he smiled, climbing into his car. As much as I hate to admit it, one of the Gray boys rescued me from humiliation.

I made my way to my car, and Brian stopped me as I was about to get in. "Are you hanging out with the Gray boys?"

"No, they're neighbors," I answered.

He rolled his eyes at me. "I'd be careful if I was you because I heard they're always in trouble. They might drag you into it."

Tricia smirked.

"I don't know where you heard that, but you're wrong."

"I'm warning you. The Gray boys' reputation is less than stellar," he remarked to me.

"Well, I've known them my entire life, and what you heard is that rumor." I couldn't stand there anymore and listen to Brian berate them. I opened the car door, tossed the bag inside, and left.

As I drove home, I don't know why, but at that moment, I felt the sudden urge to protect them.

CHAPTER 4

CAYSON GRAY

I pulled into the driveway and grabbed the plastic bag with the pads from the back seat. I got out and slammed my door, letting out a frustrated scream as I kicked my tires.

I wasn't aware someone watched me until I saw Danny and Cayson staring at me.

"It was a spider, an enormous spider." I dashed into the house.

"Your sister is weird," Cayson said to him.

"Yeah, she can be a genuine treat," Danny replied to him.

I walked in, threw the bag at Mom, and walked into my room. I was in no mood to deal with anyone.

My bedroom window was open, and I could hear the conversation between my brother and Cayson. Cayson always hung out with my brother. So, it was customary for him to be around. He was around five foot ten with black hair and grey eyes like Nate. He was the youngest of the boys and ten months more youthful than my brother.

As I kicked off my shoes, I heard Cayson say, "Did you hear your sister tried to electrocute Nate today?"

"Patty? That doesn't sound like her," my brother replied to him, confused.

"From what Nate says, she did. She was standing next to the light switch. She was trying to get even with him for blowing up her stupid dolls," he told Danny.

I sat on the side of my bed. Here I was being blamed for something I didn't even do. I also told Nate I didn't do it, then dealt with Brian in the parking lot and how I defended them. I scoffed at that thought.

When I thought things were getting better between us, they weren't. It made me wonder if Jonas was helping me or waiting to make a joke later. The thought gnawed at me.

I turned on the TV and watched some random program. I needed something to numb my mind and distract me from my thoughts.

Later on, I walked to the corner store and got something icy to drink. I could hear Nate yelling and throwing things. I hope the car hood falls on his head. I smiled at that thought.

I walked up to the store, getting a drink, and then decided some chocolate would cheer me up. I crouched down and was deciding on a candy bar. Once I made my selection, I stood up only to be face to face with Nate. He narrowed his eyes at me as I glared at him.

"You following me?" I spat at him.

"Yeah, right," he scoffed at me. He held up a bag of chips. "Ma sent me to the store."

"Whatever," was my response as I walked away.

Standing in line, another customer stood behind me, and Nate stood behind him.

"Thanks for electrocuting me," Nate accused me.

I peered around the other guy. "I already told you I didn't flip the switch."

"Then who did? The air," he replied in a testy tone.

"No, your mom," I answered as his jaw dropped, and I smirked checkmate. I paid for my stuff and left the store. Thanks to the guy behind me, taking forever, I could make the glorious escape out of the store. I would be home before Nate reached me.

Well, that was until I heard footsteps thumping against the ground. Shit. I picked up my pace until Nate reached me. He crashed into me, causing my Slurpee to fly out of my hand along with my candy bar. He flipped me over and sat on top of me.

"Can you get off of me?" I groaned at him.

"Not until you tell me the truth," he demanded.

"I told the truth! I don't lie!" I yelled at him while trying to get him off of me.

"Why would my ma do that?" He looked at me.

"How should I know? Why does Lucille do half the things she does? Now, will you get off of me?" I demanded. He climbed off of me, and I stood up. I picked up my drink, which is empty, and my candy bar. "Thanks. Thanks a lot," I said in an annoyed tone as I walked away, jerk.

CHAPTER 5

LIFE IS CRAZY THEN THERE'S LUCILLE

Senior year was a year I had waited for years — finally, the last year of high school. I was getting ready to apply to schools and graduate. I couldn't wait.

I was standing at my locker when Liz walked up and opened hers.

"You don't seem happy," I said to her.

"It is school. What's being happy about?"

"That we're finally seniors and graduating," I smiled.

"With no boyfriends," she groaned.

"Who cares? I'm fine without one all these years."

"Patty, you're not allowed to date till you were sixteen, and you have never been on a date ever," she reminded me.

"Shh," I hushed her. It was terrible enough everyone at school knew about that stupid rule. I didn't need them to know I still never had a boyfriend.

The halls were bustling with kids getting ready to start the new school year. As Liz and I were walking to class, I saw Brian make his way towards us. My heart sped up. Watching him walk, running his hand through his hair as it flopped about, made my stomach turn in knots.

He smiled that dazzling smile, and I smiled back. As he got closer to me, I thought this was it; He would talk to me. The girl he had been with would be some random girl. I opened my mouth only for him to walk past us and over to the girl; I saw him within the store.

I stood there as he kissed her, wrapping his arm around her neck. My heart shattered into a million pieces. I liked this boy for years, and all I got from him was him degrading the Gray boys. He had scolded me for knowing them.

Liz noticed my expression changed and said, "You know, he's not all that. Plus, you can always dream about the Gray boys."

I looked at her and rolled my eyes. Your friend finds out you live kitty-corner from popular guys, and that's all they talk about to you. Change that; They are not sexy. They are trouble. Bad Patty, I thought to myself.

Most of the day went along, and I walked out to my car. I passed by Brian in the parking log. He's standing next to his car with two of his buddies along with Tricia.

"I see you enjoy hanging with trash," he yelled at me.

"Excuse me?" I stopped and looked at him.

"Correct me if I'm wrong, but associating with the Gray boys makes you trash since they are." The other guys snickered.

I walked over to him. "Because you're on the football team doesn't make you better than them."

"I beg to differ. I mean, it's not like the Grays got a degree. Isn't one of them a grease monkey working on cars?"

"At least it's an honest way of life unlike you, who sponges off your girlfriend," I shot back.

He stood up and got into my face. "It's pathetic that after all these years, you can't take a hint that I won't date someone with the likes of you. You're nothing but a loser who amount to nothing, like your pathetic excuse of neighbors."

That's when I lost it. I hauled off and slapped Brian across the face. That pissed him off, and he ended up punching me in the face. I fell to the ground.

"Brian! What the hell, man?" One of his buddies yelled at him as I tried to hold my composure.

"No one puts their hands on me," he barked to them. He grabbed my face and looked at me. "That's only a taste. You're a piece of trash," he growled at me, then shoved my face back.

He walked away as the others followed. I reached up to see blood. Grabbing a shirt from my bag, I held it to my nose. Danny hit me before when I was roughhousing with him, but nothing like this.

I got up and staggered over to my car. I opened the door, getting inside, and held the shirt to my nose. I pulled out of the school parking lot and drove home. I needed to get back and pass Mom without her seeing me.

I pulled up front and turned off the car. I got out as Cayson tapped Nate and pointed to me. He pulled his head out from under the hood of the car and looked at me.

"What the hell?" Nate asked, looking at me, holding the bloody shirt to my face.

"I know she's a klutz and all, but that doesn't look right," Cayson remarked to him.

"Stay here," he said as he walked over to me. "Patty?"

I looked at him while still holding the shirt to my nose. "Oh, hey, Nate," I said.

"What happened?" He nodded to the bloody shirt.

"It's a nosebleed," I lied to him, not wanting to tell him the truth or cry in front of him, even though my face hurt, and I wanted to.

"Uh-huh, sure, let me see," he reached for the shirt I held.

"It's fine," I lied again, trying not to let Nate take the shirt from me.

"Let me check it," he said, pulling the shirt from me, "Jesus."

"I'm fine," I lied.

"No, you're not. Come on, let's get you cleaned up."

"I won't win this argument, will I?"

"Nope," he answered.

I sighed. "Okay, but I need to call Mom. The last time I didn't tell her where I was, she about shook my head off."

He chuckled. "I remember that. That was some funny shit."

"Yeah, for others, it wasn't so much for me."

We walked over to his house and inside. He had Lucille call my mom while he cleaned me up.

"It's Lucille, Joan. Yeah, I had Patty stopover to help me with something. Yeah, she's helping me lance a boil on Nate's butt."

We poked our head out of the bathroom, looked at her, and then looked at each other as we mouthed to each other, "Boil?"

"Yeah, I'll send her home when we get done. Okay, bye," she hung up.

I swear that woman lies more than a dog.

I sat on the toilet lid while Nate sat on the side of the tub, cleaning up my face.

"So, want to tell me who did this?" He pressed me.

"I already said, I got a bloody nose."

"You're a terrible liar. Trust me; my ma is the queen of bullshit."

"I've noticed," I agreed as he finished cleaning me up. He put the first aid kit back while he sat back down and looked at me.

"Come on, Patty, tell me," he coaxed me.

I took a deep breath. "It was Brian."

"What?" He looked at me, not only stunned but angry.

"He was saying a bunch of stuff about you guys, and I got mad, so I slapped him. Then he hit me. Told me no one touches him," I explained, trying not to cry.

"Oh," he stood up, his fist clenched, and his jaw tightened.

"Nate, please don't. He's not worth it." I reached up, grabbing his hand, looking at him with pleading eyes. I knew his temper, and I knew he would knock out Brian's teeth.

He let out a sigh. "Fine, but if he touches you again, I'll touch him, starting with his teeth."

He walked away, and I stood up. I looked in the mirror. My nose was bruising but not broken, and bruising appeared under my eyes. God, I needed to cover this up.

I walked out of the bathroom and into the kitchen. "Do you have any cover-up, Lucille?"

"Sure do. Come on," Lucille said to me as I followed her into her bedroom. She helped me hide the bruising until I could get past my mom. "Now, who did this?"

I tried to think of an excuse.

"Never mind, I already heard your conversation with Nate."

"You were listening?"

"I call it selective eavesdropping," she smirked because that's what she did.

I sat on the bed and let out a deep sigh. Lucille sat down next to me.

"Look, I know people think low of my boys. Hell, I think low of my boys." I gave her a look. "But they're my boys. I gave birth to them so I may think whatever I like."

"It's that people don't know them. To hear the way people bash them makes me angry. I couldn't help myself."

"Sure, you could. You could have come home, told the boys, and they would have beaten his ass the right way," she reasoned.

"Lucille, he's seventeen. They could go to jail," I reasoned.

"I got bail money," she shrugged. I swear she was something else.

"Look, I got to go. Thanks for the concealer." I waved to her as I walked out of her bedroom and out of the house. I waved to Nate and Cayson as I walked over to my house.

Lucille came outside. "Well," Nate asked her.

"Damn shame, he put his hands on her," she remarked to them.

"Why?" Cayson asked her.

"Because you boys take care of him."

"We are?" They both questioned her.

"Yep, and Nate, I want you to take her to school," she suggested.

"Why? She has a car," he reminded her.

"Yeah, that won't start." She winked at him.

He gave her a look and shook his head. She went back inside.

"Ma's crazy," Cayson remarked to Nate.

"Psh, you need not remind me," Nate said, letting out a deep breath.

Later on that night, he and Cayson ran over to my car, and he climbed underneath.

"Hand me that flashlight," Nate ordered Cayson.

Cayson handed him the flashlight. He turned it on, shining it underneath my car, looking for something. Once he found out what he was looking for, he pulled the wire.

He hurried out from underneath the car and got up. They ran back over to their house.

"Good thing you know about cars," Cayson said to him.

"Yeah, or this would end badly. I swear ma is trying to get me killed," Nate said back to him.

"What else is new?" He smirked as they both laughed.

Yep, thanks to Lucille, my life was about to get interesting.

CHAPTER 6

CAR PROBLEMS

I walked out to my car to go to school when I climbed in and tried to start it, but nothing. It wouldn't even turn over. Damn it. I didn't have time for this.

I got out of the car and looked at my watch. I could walk, which would take me a few more minutes longer than I did. I debated this for a minute. Then I heard someone yell, "Car trouble?"

I turned to see Nate walking out to his car.

"Yeah! I don't know what the problem is!" I yelled back.

"Well, I'm passing by the school if you want a ride?" He offered.

I stood there and thought about it. Eh, why not? Better than walking. I walked over to his car and got into it. He climbed into the driver's side, and once my seatbelt fastened; He pulled out of the driveway.

We didn't talk much unless he said he would look at my car when he got a chance. Nate was a funny character. We used to discuss all the time; Then something changed between us. I didn't know what it was.

He pulled into the parking lot, and I got out. I thanked him for the ride, and he left. Liz met up with me as I walked into the school.

"Was that Nate Gray?" She asked with a grin.

"Yeah, he gave me a ride to school."

"You are lucky," she said with a sigh.

"Only because my car wouldn't start," I told her.

Then she did a double-take when she saw my face. "What happened to your face?"

"A door," I lied to her.

"Huh?" She looked at me.

"I ran into a door in the middle of the night," I know she wanted to press me for answers, but I didn't want to talk about it. Getting punch by a guy was bad enough, but it be your crush was ten times worse. All because I defended the Gray boys.

Most of the day, I tried to avoid Brian, but that was easier said than done. He caught me in the parking lot — round 2.

"Leave me alone," I said, trying to get past him.

"Aw, is someone mad because she got what she deserved? Didn't your parents ever teach you that if you raise your hand to someone, then they may defend themselves? I was defending myself," he smirked as the other guys surrounded me.

The second day of school, and I get to deal with this. Well, that was until I heard someone yell, "Patty!"

We all turned to see Nate and Cayson standing there, leaning against Nate's car.

I waved. "Hey, guys!"

"Come on, your mom is waiting," Nate yelled.

I looked at Brian. "Excuse me; my ride is here."

As I walked past them, Brian stuck out his foot and tripped me.

"How was your trip? See you next fall." He laughed, as did the others. That was it; I was sick of him.

Cayson looked at Nate. "Should we help her?"

"Let's see what she can do. I mean, she had us growing up," Nate said to Cayson as they both watched me.

I got up and walked towards him. Then I pulled my fist back and let it rip. I punched him right in the nose. "That's for hitting me!"

He looked at me, and I hit him again. "That's for tripping me!"

Then I kneed him in the junk. "And that's for being the biggest douche that walked the face of the earth."

"Ooh," Nate and Cayson said, wincing.

"The Gray boys may not be much to anyone else. Thanks to them, I can take care of myself, and they don't treat me like garbage," I spat at him. I don't think Brian realized that I was a tomboy growing up and getting into scuffles with my brother and the Gray boys.

I picked up my bag and walked towards Nate's car. "You know, if you keep hanging around them, you won't go anywhere," Tricia yelled.

I turned back around and looked at her. "I'll go further than you think. At least with them, what you see is what you get!" With that, I walked over to Nate and Cayson.

"I've got to hand it to you," Nate said, looking at his fingers as he had his other hand in his pockets.

"What?" I looked at him.

"You can at least handle yourself," he answered as a smile grew on his lips.

"I hope so. Growing up with you guys and brother, I had to learn how to fend for myself," I said with a smile.

He leaned over and whispered, "Yeah, but you shouldn't have to." I felt his fiery breath on my cheek, and my heart sped up. I looked at him in the eyes. My blue eyes are meeting his grey eyes. There was something in them that made me realize; There was more than what either of us wanted to admit. That scared me.

I climbed into the backseat as they got into the front. Nate pulled out of the school parking lot and drove home. He pulled into his driveway, and I got out. I waved to them and walked across the street to my house.

"You like her," Cayson commented.

"What? Don't be ridiculous. She's Danny's little sister," he said.

"Doesn't mean you can't like her," he shrugged.

"She's seventeen," Nate responded, trying to find a reason not to like me.

"And she'll be eighteen. What's your point?" Cayson reasoned with him.

"My point is, she has all these plans," he said, waving his hand around.

"Yeah, so?"

"So, it's not happening," Nate answered as he walked away. Then Jonas walked up.

"What's up with Nathan?"

"He won't admit he likes Patty," Cayson shrugged.

"Well, he is delusional," Jonas smirked.

"I know that, and you know that, but he won't admit that," Cayson retorted.

"Did it ever dawn on him that if he doesn't make a move, ma kills him?" Jonas asked Cayson.

"Do you think he cares?"

"Good point," Jonas agreed with him.

"Boys," they heard a gruff voice as the person walked up.

"Dad," they greeted him.

"Jonas, they need you at this location tomorrow at seven am," he said, handing Jonas an address.

"Great," Jonas sighed, looking at the address.

Grayson looked at Cayson. "Found a job yet?"

"I'm working on it," Cayson mumbled.

"Work faster," Grayson ordered him, and with that, he walked away.

"You know there's still that opening for that manufacturing plant," Jonas suggested to him.

"Yeah, I know. I'll call the people tomorrow," Cayson said, letting out a sigh.

Grayson walked in and kissed Lucille. Nate came walking into the kitchen after showering and changing.

"Nathaniel," Grayson acknowledged Nate.

"Dad," Nate said.

They say not much between father and son. When you are similar in personality, things are a little tense.

"How's dinner coming?" Grayson asked Lucille.

"It's almost cook," she said to him. He let out a groan. "Gray, it won't get done any faster if you mope about here. Now go clean up," she ordered him.

"Fine," he responded as he went into the bathroom to wash up.

"So, how was your little expedition with Patty?" Lucille asked Nate.

"The girl can handle herself, that's for sure."

"She should consider how rough you three boys and her brother are on her," she smirked.

"That guy is such an asshole," he mumbled.

"What guy?"

"Brian Holloway thinks he's better than everyone because he's dating the Holcomb girl," he snapped.

She handed him plates to set the table.

"Is he an asshole because he's dating that girl or because it infatuates Patty with him?" She asked him.

He gave her a look. "What does that have to do with anything?"

"Everything," she said.

I had dinner and caught up with some television. Yes, I lead an exciting life.

I lay on my bed, thinking about what happened today after school. Hitting Brian twice in the face and then kneeing him in the groin gave me a satisfaction I didn't know was possible.

I liked him for years, but everyone kept telling me what a douche he was. I thought they were all being petty until he made me a target. Then anger boiled inside of me, thinking about it. I found very few guys attractive at school. I usually found one. Developed a crush, then got crushed — such a nasty cycle.

As I laid on my bed replaying the day's events, I heard someone tap on my window outside, scaring the living shit out of me. I got up and looked through the screen.

"Nate?"

"I thought I would replace the Slurpee. I caused you to drop when I tackled you," he said. He held up two Slurpees.

"How much do you think I can drink?"

He gave me a look, pursing his lips into a straight line. "One's for me, dumbass," he answered.

I gave him a confused look. "Oh," I replied.

"Are you going to come and get it, or I have to give it to Cayson?"

"No, no, I'll be out in a minute," I answered his impatient ass as I grabbed a hoodie and pulled it on. It was still warm outside, but the nights were getting colder.

I walked out of the back door of the house. He was sitting on the picnic table with the Slurpee next to him. I climbed up and took a seat next to him. I picked up the Slurpee and took a sip. Ah, frozen, sugary goodness hit my tongue and slipped down my throat.

Then it happened, brain freeze.

"Ah!"

He laughed as I held my head. "Stop laughing. It's not funny," I said, giving him a playful slap.

"It's a little funny," he gestured with his finger and thumb.

After my brain freeze went away, we sat there and slurped our Slurpees in silence.

"I miss this," he said with a deep sigh.

"What? Getting brain freeze?"

"No, when I used to hang out with you and talk."

"You talked to me through my bedroom window while coming by to see Danny. I hardly consider that as hanging out and talking," I reminded him.

"Yeah, but it was still nice."

"Yeah, it was," I said with a sigh. Then I checked my watch. "Got to go. School comes way too early."

"Miss the summer, don't ya?"

"Not having to deal with jerks and getting up early, always. Night Nate," I said to him.

"Night, Patty," he said back to me.

With that, I got ready for bed. I turned off the TV and light, then snuggled into my blankets. I drifted off to sleep. I thought about were those nights when Nate talked to me through my bedroom window during the summer.

A smile curled upon my lips.

CHAPTER 7

LATE NIGHT CHATS

After that night of sharing a Slurpee with Nate, I went along with my business. That meant school and my part-time job. I was trying to save for school. I know that a scholarship help, and grants too, but I needed to make up the difference.

The only difference was, every evening, I would hear a tap on my windowsill, only to find Nate standing there. The light from my window would show part of him while the night would hide the rest. If it weren't for a cast of view, I wouldn't know who it was.

Every night was something different from him. Looking for my brother, he's bored, so forth and so on. I didn't mind. We ended up talking about everything and nothing at the same time. It reminded me of when I was younger with him.

"I miss this," he said.

"Miss what?" I asked him.

"Our talks, you could always make me laugh," he said.

"Yep, I'm a real comedian," I grinned.

"What changed?" He looked at me, and I looked up at the sky, thinking.

"You got a girlfriend, or should I say several, but then again, our lives got busy."

"Yeah," he said.

"I got to go. It's getting late," I said to Nate as I climbed off of the picnic table and walked towards the house.

"It's a Friday." He looked at me with a smirk.

"What can I say? I'm getting old." I turned to face him with a shrug.

I walked inside, leaving him out there alone. Once inside my room, I heard the grass move. I looked out of my window, and he left. I couldn't help but smile at that.

I was sleeping when something hit me.

"What the hell?" I woke up startled.

"Mom has been calling you for the past ten minutes," Danny said, annoyed, standing at my doorway.

I fell back onto my pillow, face down, "It's Saturday," I said with a muffled sound.

"And it's a mom. What's your point?" He shrugged.

"My point is to get out," I yelled, picking up a shoe and throwing it at him. It hit the door frame and bounced off.

"All those times playing catch, and you still have no control over you're pitching," he teased me.

"Get out," I growled. Danny shrugged and left.

It's Saturday, the day of no school and naps. Don't judge. I like my naps.

"Patty!" Mom yelled.

"What?" I yelled back.

"Are you going to sleep all day?"

"Yes," I whined.

I looked at the clock, and it was nine in the morning. Ugh, I'm a teen. I'm supposed to stay up all night and sleep all day. Well, not in this house.

I dragged my butt out of bed and went to the bathroom. Luckily, I didn't have far to go, since it was right next to my room and I had to turn the corner.

After the bathroom, I walked into the kitchen, yawning.

"Nice PJs," I heard a voice comment.

I looked forward, and to my horror was Nate standing in my kitchen. I looked down to see that I was only in a nightshirt and shorts. He smirked, and I bolted to my room, slamming the door shut.

What the hell was he doing here?

I grabbed a robe and threw it on. If Dad found out I was roaming around in my PJs around the neighbor boy, I would never hear the end. Trust me; The "talk" didn't go well.

I opened my door to hear Nate say, "Ready?"

Ready for what?

"Yeah, let me grab my jacket," Danny said. He was here for my brother.

They left, and Nate acted like I didn't even exist, unlike this past week when we talked, figures.

I slumped down in a kitchen chair, and Mom made me a plate of food.

"Is there a reason you're moody?" She asked me while setting the plate in front of me.

"No," I grumbled.

"Uh-huh," she said to me as she went back to doing dishes while I ate. I don't understand. Nate's talking and laughing with me; The next, he acts like I don't even exist. I'll never understand, guys.

I had met many guys. After I turned sixteen, another friend from school tried to fix me up with many unique guys. It's like an alarm went off announcing I could date.

They all turned out to be duds, and I had to wonder if I didn't have a big L on my forehead for the word loser. That's when Dad had the "talk" at dinner. Thank God for Mom because he failed.

Life with guys was rough, and so was my non-existent dating life. I'll hibernate in my room until I'm old and too tired to care.

"Are you even listening to me, Patty?" Liz asked me, breaking me from my thoughts.

"Huh?" I looked at her, confused.

"I guess not," Liz sighed. "What is wrong with you?" She pokes my forehead twice.

"It's nothing. I'll die old and alone," I shrugged.

"I thought you were okay being single?" she asked me, raising her eyebrows.

I sat up and looked at her. Liz had been my best friend our entire life. She had dark curly hair, green eyes, and legs that went on for miles. She was stunning and could get any guy she wanted. I wasn't. I was of average height, size and had light brown hair with blue eyes.

"Liz, will you look at me? Does it look like any guy is beating down my door? No," I spoke.

"Well, they would if you weren't picky," she giggled.

I gave her a look. "Be serious."

"Okay, so you and Nate hung out every evening this past week. Was there any spark?"

"I doubt it. The dude is way older, and I doubt he sees me as anything more than a sister. Today, he said, 'Nice pj's' and that was it," I said, mocking him.

"That's harsh," she snickered.

"Liz!" I exclaimed.

"Patty!" she said in a mocking tone.

"Come on; I'm serious. Homecoming is coming up, and once again, I'm stuck home while you're out having fun," I pouted to her.

"Well, you would have fun if you came with me instead of sitting at home." She rolled her eyes at me.

"And play the third wheel to you and your date, no thank you."

"Well, why you ponder your life choices or their lack, I have to go home."

"Fine."

"Later haters," she said as she left my bedroom.

"Later," I told her.

It's another homecoming where I stay home once again, yippee.

Liz walked out of my house, and someone yanked her by the arm. "Ack!"

"Shh, keep your voice down," Cayson shushed her.

"No need to yank my arm out of its socket," she said, rubbing her arm.

"So, what did she say?" Jonas asked her.

"She gets a bunch of cats and become a cat lady."

"Are you serious?" Jonas asked her.

She rolled her eyes. "No," she answered.

"Oh," he said.

"For someone that's supposed to be so smart, you're dumb," she remarked to Jonas.

"Who cares? We can discuss Jonas being dumb another time," Cayson said with an annoyed tone.

"Hey!"

"Relax, dumb ass. Ma sent us on a mission," Cayson rolled his eyes.

"Can you two bicker like an old married couple later?" she asked them.

They both gave her a look as she shrugged.

"Look, we need to get those two together before ma kills Nate," Cayson said to her.

"What?" She looked at him like he was crazy.

"Trust us; It's not pretty. Ma wants them together," Jonas said to her.

"Shouldn't they make that decision?" She asked them.

"Have you met our ma?" Cayson asked her. "She's nuts."

Jonas nodded in agreement.

She looked at both of them. "Fine, I guess they have been talking, but Nate acted like it was nothing, which means Patty thinks she won't ever find a guy."

"Why do girls always think the worse?" Jonas asked her.

"Dude, girls always think the worse. It's like something ingrained in them," Cayson said to him.

"We're female. We have a bunch of hormones. You deal with bleeding for a week straight, and all the other bullshit that goes with it telling me how you feel."

"Ew, we didn't need to know all that," they said with a look of disgust.

"Then don't discuss women, you dink," she shot back.

"Look, our brother is an idiot. We all know this. We also know Patty has had a thing for him her entire life. Now we need to push them together," Cayson said. Jonas nodded in agreement.

"Fine. If this blows up in our faces, you're blind." Liz pointed to Cayson. "You're deaf." She looked at Jonas. "And I don't know either you."

"Fine," Cayson said.

My door opened, and they ran through the driveway, ducking out of view. I stopped and looked around. Huh, I shrugged and went to get the mail.

As I walked back looking at the mail, I heard someone yell, "Hey, trash girl!" I looked up. Brian and his cronies pelted me with tomatoes. I dropped the mail, which caused it to scattered all over the ground.

They laughed and sped off. I stood there and pulled the residue of the tomatoes off of me. I couldn't help it as I cry, then I picked up my mail and wiped the tears from my cheeks.

Cayson, Jonas, and Liz watched me. I walked over to my steps and sat down. I placed my head in my hands and cried, letting the mail drop to my feet.

Liz looked at them. "All she did, defend you guys, and since then, he has been making her life hell. Do you think that's fair?"

They looked at her and then at me, "No, it's cruel."

"Exactly, imagined if this blows up how much crueler it is to her. I know your mom means well, but if this doesn't work out, it crushes her," she said, walking away.

I wiped my eyes, refusing to cry. Nate pulled into the driveway with Danny. Danny got out and walked up to me.

"Patty?" He looked me up and down. "What happened?"

"Nothing," I answered him.

"Doesn't look like nothing," he furrowed his brows.

"It's nothing. Leave it," I said, getting up and going inside. Nate sat in his car and gripped his steering wheel as he watches Danny follow me inside.

He knew who did this.

CHAPTER 8

LIFE IS FULL OF LEMONS

Nate was fuming at the thought of what happened to me. He knew who had done it. He was sure of it, but he had to wait. I was right. Age was a significant factor. But the minute he got a chance, he would show Brian who not to mess with me.

I went to the bathroom and stripped off my clothes, letting the tomato ridden clothes fall to the floor. I turned on the shower until it was hot enough and climbed in.

A skunk had sprayed if it would have been one thing. I would have welcomed someone pelting me with tomatoes to rid me of the stench, but I wasn't.

No, all I was lucky enough was to have a guy I like throw tomatoes at me and laugh. Then have Danny and Nate pull into the driveway only to stare at like I was some freak. The thought irked me.

I washed all the tomatoes off me and washed my hair twice until I was sure it was off me. I turned off the shower and got out, drying myself then wrapping a towel around me.

I rubbed the mirror with my hand and stared at my reflection. Was I that bad? Was I not attractive? I let out a deep sigh. It didn't matter. No matter what I did, it would never be good enough.

I walked into my room and over to my dresser, pulling out clothes. I was so focused on other things I didn't notice someone in my room.

I turned and yelled, "Jesus!"

"Not quite," he smirked.

"Get out!" I demanded. He gave me a look. "Out! If my parents find you in here, they have a flipping cow!"

"They're not home. Your parents went over to your grandma's house." Great, thanks, Mom and Dad. "But I'll leave so you can get dressed, then we talk."

He got up and walked out of the room, closing the door behind him. I threw on a shirt, sweats, and socks. I walked over to my door and opened it. He was standing in the small hallway, waiting for me.

I stepped aside and waved him back in. He walked in and took a seat on my bed, tossing my wet towel on a chair. I sat down next to him.

"Okay. Talk," Nate ordered.

"What's talking about?" I shrugged.

"I know Brian did that to you."

I looked at him, and he was serious.

"Nate, it's fine."

"No, it's not."

"Yes, it is," I said with seriousness to my tone.

"Patty, it's not fine. It's cruel."

I could see the anger boiling inside him, and it was a little scary.

"Nate, with people like Brian, is there is another one to take their place," I said.

"That's the problem; people accept that behavior."

I couldn't help but think he was right. I mean, has it become so acceptable that people would sooner accept it than do something about it?

"I know what people think of us. It's not an unknown fact." He told me.

"But you do nothing about it. Isn't that as bad?" I asked him.

It was a simple question. I mean, if you say other people's behavior is terrible, is knowing it's awful worse?

"Nope," Nate answered with a shrug.

"How so?"

"Because it's gossip. Gossip is a ninety-nine percent false statement and one percent truth. Have we gotten into trouble? Yeah, but we also do dumb things that warrant it."

"That makes no sense," I said, getting up and walking over to my dresser. It's like Nate accepted people talking about them and bad-mouthing them.

I picked up a hairbrush and started brushing my hair.

"It need not make sense."

I stopped and turned to him. "What?"

He stood up and walked over to me. "It need not make sense. While there is one person out there that thinks bad of us, there is one person in here that doesn't."

He looked at me in the eyes when he said that. I couldn't help but become uncomfortable with it. I maneuvered around him and sat back on my bed.

"Look, I'm saying that there is no reason for him to do this," he said to me.

I didn't know what to say. It was like we were going around in circles with it. I felt the need to protect them, and Nate felt the need to protect me. I didn't know why?

Nate left my house and gathered up his brothers.

"Explain this to me again," Cayson said to him.

"We're going to go talk with Brian. With our fists," he said.

"Suitable explanation," Cayson agreed with Nate.

As they got into the car, Lucille ran out to his car window and said, "Do I need bail money?"

Nate looked at her. "I hope not."

With that, he started the car, and they pulled out their driveway. They drove over to Brian's house and parked out in front of his home on the street. The three of them got out of the car and strolled up to the front door.

Nate rang the bell, and as soon as Brian opened the door, Nate's fist met him, causing him to fall back. He grabbed his nose, yelping in pain. Nate walked through the door with Jonas and Cayson following behind him.

"I'll only say this once, leave Patty George alone. If I find out you're bothering her anymore, the next time worse."

Brian propped himself up and looked at him while holding his nose.

"While you're calling us trash, you don't understand; You're the real trash. You're hanging onto a rich girlfriend, strutting around like you're better than anyone else. That not only makes you trash but pathetic. Stay away from her," he growled as he turned and walked away.

"Yeah, I would do what he says. You wouldn't want to see him pissed," Jonas smirked as he turned to leave with Cayson shrugging.

They walked back to the car and got inside.

"Well, at least we didn't need bail money," Cayson said to them.

"Unless his parents call the cops and press charges for assault," Jonas said.

"They won't press charges because if they did, then she can press charges against their boy for assault," Nate said. He drove home.

I was in my room watching TV when I noticed red and blue lights flash outside of my bedroom window. Since my room was in the back, I went to the front to find out what was going on. Police are stopping someone from speeding.

I got to the front door to see Mom standing there and Danny walking up.

"Well," she asked him.

"Nate hit some kid," he said to her.

"What do you mean he hit a kid?" I asked, confused.

"I guess he went to some kid's house and not only hit him but threaten him. The police are here to arrest him," he shrugged.

Oh, hell no, I knew who it was. I walked past Mom and towards the Gray house.

"Where are you going?" She yelled after me.

"To take a stand," I yelled back. My mom and brother ran after me.

I walked up to see Grayson fuming and Lucille speaking to the cops while Nate sat in the back like a common criminal. I took a deep breath and walked over to the police. "Excuse me."

He turned and looked at me. "Yes," he answered.

"There has been a misunderstanding."

"Young lady, this doesn't concern you," the police officer chided.

"But it does."

They all stopped and looked at me while Mom and my brother finally reached me.

"Here we go," Jonas mumbled as he looked up.

I walked over to the cop with Lucille. "See, the boy that reported Nathaniel Gray isn't as innocent as he claims to be."

"What do you mean?" The police officer questioned me.

I took another deep breath and wet my lips. I was a ball of nerves and could feel my adrenaline coursing through my body.

"I mean, the boy that reported Nate, well, he hit me," I admitted to the cop.

All their jaws dropped.

"Do you have any proof of this?" The officer asked me.

"His friends and girlfriend were there and saw it happened. If you ask them, they lie, but I don't. Now the question is, do you have any proof of Nate hitting him?"

"Miss, that's none of your concern."

"It is. Because unless you have concrete proof, Nate was at Brian's house, then it's his word against Nate's." I shrugged.

"Look, the kid is claiming he was at his house."

"What time?" I asked the officer.

"What?"

"What time was he at his house?"

"He claims it was 5:15 in the evening. Why?"

"Because he was actually at my house," I lied.

"Do you have any proof?"

"Yes, she does. Nate was over because we were all hanging out," Danny added, backing me up.

The officer looked at us then at Nate's parents, as Lucille said, "There you go, officer. I told you my boy was at the neighbors."

We looked at her, and she shot us a glance. Okay, that was weird. Lucille said he was at our house, and we corroborated her story. We've been hanging around the Gray boys too long.

The officers looked at each other and conversed about the situation. Then one came over to me. "Do you want to press charges against the boy that hit you?"

"No, as long as he leaves the Grays alone, I won't press charges," I said in a soft voice.

"Very well," the officer looked at his partner. "Release him. We'll pay a visit to one Brian Holloway."

The other officer nodded, letting Nate out, and they all got back into their cars and pulled out. He looked at me, as did the rest of them as I turned while walking away, not saying a word.

I don't know why I did what I did tonight. I guess the conversation Nate and I had earlier stuck with me. I didn't want things to stay how they were; I wanted them to change.

CHAPTER 9

CONSPIRACY THEORIES

I don't know what happened between Nate and Brian, but Brian kept his distance from me. I was thankful for that. I stood in the school's hallway, looking at the flyers plaster on the wall announcing homecoming. I would not be attending because I never went to school dances.

Who would I go with to homecoming? It's not like I had many options.

"So, you're telling me you would rather stay home and clean your room then go to a dance?" Liz looked at me, dumbfounded. What was wrong with having a nice clean room?

"You are not staying home," she demanded.

"No offense, but it's not like I have guys beating down my door," I snapped at her.

"I could ask Keith if he has a friend," she suggested with a cheesy smile.

"And be a charity case? No, thanks," I said, putting my hand out to emphasize a no. I didn't want people to feel sorry for me. I wanted a guy to ask me because he wanted to.

I slammed my locker door shut and walked away. I'm over talking about this. Liz left and made a call. She tossed some money into a phone slot of a payphone and dialed a phone number. "Hey, it's me. I got some news. Meet me at Dominick's party store. Who cares if I'm skipping? Meet me there." She hung up and checked to make sure the coast was clear and started walking to Dominick's.

It took about ten minutes for her to reach the party store. She walked up to see Cayson in the parking lot leaning against his car.

"What took you so long?" He asked her as she walked up to him.

"Unlike you, I had to walk. Usually, I get a ride from someone, but everyone is in class," Liz said, rolling her eyes at Cayson.

"Yeah, because you're a rebel and don't go to class," he smirked.

"Well, at least when I graduate, I have prospects," she smirked back.

"Whatever, I start a job tomorrow. So, what is this so-called news?"

"Patty needs a date."

"Why and for what?"

"It's for Homecoming. She shouldn't be sitting home, cleaning her room for the umpteenth time," she said, raising a finger at him.

He pursed his lips into a thin line and crossed his arms across his chest. "Even if that's true, there is no way Nate would go to a school dance. He doesn't like dances."

"Have you asked him?"

"He's my brother. I have never seen him attend a dance in his entire life. It's not like I can walk up to him and say, 'Hey Nate, how about taking Patty to a dance?' He would laugh," he said, raising his eyebrows.

"Suitable point," she said, shaking her finger at him. Then she started playing with her lips as she thought about it. Finally, she said, "I got it. You take her."

"What? No!" He waved his hands back and forth. "No way!"

"Oh, come on, be a pal!" Liz exclaimed.

"That would take my sister to the dance! Gross!"

She stared at him and shook her head as a giggle escaped her lips.

"What's so funny?" He asked unamused.

"What's funny is that if you take her to homecoming, then Nate takes more of an interest in her. When he does, he may get his shit together and ask her out?" She said to him twirling her finger around, hoping he got the point?

"I doubt it. I have yet seen Nate get jealous over Patty," he scoffed.

"Because no one has been a threat. Think about it. No guy has shown an interest in her. That means there's never been a threat or a reason he can't have her," she said, arching an eyebrow.

He stood there and thought about it. Liz was right; There wasn't a threat. Why would Nate pursue someone if there wasn't a challenge? The whole situation was simple. They needed to make it complicated.

"I'll do you one better," he said, waving his finger at her. "I'll get Jonas to do it."

"The dude is like fifty," she said.

"Twenty-two, but I let him know you think he's old," he smirked.

"Whatever. Make sure Jonas asks Patty," she said as she left to walk back to school. He watched as she walked away with her curls bounced upon her shoulders.

He got into his car and drove home. It could go either way. Either Nate makes a move, or this puts a wedge between the brothers. But if it involved their ma, it would go exactly how they wanted it to with Nate and me.

I got out of school, driving home. I needed to get ready for work. That was one beautiful thing about a part-time job. It kept me busy, plus I made money.

While I got ready for work, Cayson was conspiring against me with none other than his mother.

"I knew you were the smarter of the three," she said, tapping her finger against her lips.

"I figured if I talk to Jonas and get him on the same page, then it would help motivate Nate," Cayson said to her.

"Fine, but this is between you, me, and Jonas. Nate can be so stubborn like your father," she grumbled.

"Why are you so bent on getting them together?" He asked her.

"Because sometimes a mother knows what's best for her children even when they don't know it themselves," she said. She walked away to take care of the laundry.

Jonas walked into the house and was on his way to his room when Cayson dragged him into his bedroom. "Really? I just got home," he said to him.

"Yes, because we got bigger plans than you needing to wash your ass," he commented as he rubbed his hands together.

He gave Cayson a look. "Why do I get a feeling that I dislike this?"

Cayson smirked and arched his eyebrow at him.

"Are you serious?" Jonas exclaimed.

"It's perfect. Think about it, Patty goes to homecoming, Nate finally gets a clue, and ma is happy. You want ma to be happy, don't you?" Jonas furrowed his brows at Cayson. He hated it when he used the happy mom card.

"Then, Nate punches me because he has a temper. Did you forget that scenario?" He placed his hands on his waist and glared at him.

Cayson's door opened, and Lucille walked into the room, closing the door behind her.

"Well," she asked.

"He doesn't want to do it," Cayson said as a matter of fact.

"Why not?" She inquired with a disapproving tone.

"Because I don't want to feel Nate's fist," Jonas shot back.

"Who cares?"

His expression changed to shock. "I care."

She shrugged.

"I don't believe this!" He turned around and walked over to Cayson's bed, taking a seat on edge. He ran his hand through his hair in frustration.

"Jonas, Nathaniel won't hit you, but this gets his ass in gear," she said.

"And if he does?" He asked her.

"Then, I have no choice to take him in hand."

They both looked at her. "Never mind. Ask Patty to the dance and let me take care of Nathaniel," she said.

While those three conspired against me, I was working a shift at the local grocery store. As I stocked the shelves, I heard someone say, "Excuse me, miss. Could you help me?"

I looked up to see Nate leaning against a shelf with one hand. I stood up and looked at him. "Isn't it bad enough? Do I have to deal with you across the street? Now you feel the need to stalk me at my place of work?"

"I'm bored," he shrugged.

"Did you get off work?" I asked, looking at his clothing that was dirty and had grease all over it.

"Yep," Nate answered.

"Then go home and take a shower. You smell like a garage," I said.

"Adds to my charm," he smirked.

I gave him a look and rolled my eyes until I heard someone clear their throat. I turned to see my boss standing there with his hands on his hips, giving me a disapproving look, great.

I smiled at him and turned to Nate. "Either buy something or leave. You get me fired," I whispered.

He rolled his eyes. "Fine, I'll see you around." I watched him walk away and did a palm wave to my boss as I got back to work. I swear those Gray boys are the death of me yet.

CHAPTER 10

TO HOMECOMING OR NOT TO HOMECOMING, THAT IS THE QUESTION?

Homecoming, one of the significant dances at school, has about a month after school starts. Ours is usually around the end of September. I always end up missing it because a guy doesn't ask me.

Most girls would go with each other in a group, but if I danced, I would like to go with someone to at least slow dance.

I did what I usually do and clean my room. Might as well be productive.

As I contemplated my non-existent love life, there was a knock at the front door.

"Patty! Someone's here to see you," Mom yelled for me. That was odd.

I went to the front door, and there stood Jonas. I opened the door and stepped out, letting the screen door close behind me.

"Jonas? What's going on?" I asked him, confused.

"Hey, Patty, did you want to go to the homecoming dance?" It was a simple request, and I looked past him to see Lucille and Cayson trying to act casual. What in the world?

I turned my attention back to him.

"Aren't you too old to be going to school dances?" I asked Jonas, confused.

"You're never too old to go to a dance," he said with a wink and a smile.

I sighed. "Don't do that. It's creepy."

"What this?" He winked again.

"Yes, that. It's creepy."

He chuckled. "So, what do you say?"

I thought about it for a minute. The idea appealed to me. It would grind Brian to see one of the Gray boys escort me to Homecoming. I wouldn't be sitting home again like the other times, hmmm.

"Fine, I'll go to the dance with you," I accepted his request.

"Great," he smiled.

He turned and walked away as I went back into the house. I couldn't believe it. I was going to Homecoming and not alone, with one of the Gray boys no less, oh boy.

Jonas walked towards his brother and mother and said, "She said yes!"

"Who said yes?" Nate asked, coming out of the house.

"Oh, Patty, I asked her to homecoming, and she agreed," he grinned.

Nate looked at him and raised an eyebrow. "Aren't you too old to be going to school dances?"

"You're never too old to take a pretty girl to a dance," he shrugged, earning a look from Nate. With those words, he, Cayson, and Lucille walked into the house.

Once inside, Jonas asked, "Do you think he bought it?"

"Oh, he bought it," Cayson answered.

"Well, if he would get his ass in gear, he would take her instead of you," Lucille said to Jonas.

"You know he'll kill us when he finds out what we're doing," Jonas said to them.

"Eh, live a little," Cayson shrugged.

I couldn't believe it. I was going to my first school dance in years, and it was with Jonas Gray of all people, enjoyable.

I knew I needed a dress so, whom do I call? That would be none other than my best friend. Her screams pierced my eardrums when I told her about Jonas, asking me to the dance.

I never got the whole screaming bit us girls make when we're excited about something. I don't think I ever let out a scream like that, but I have never been very enthusiastic about anything.

Liz and I went dress shopping for a dress for Homecoming. I found an emerald-colored dress, but that got vetoed. Next was purple, nope. Red? Yeah, I don't think so. Orange? Yuck, and I was running out of ideas and colors.

"Patty! I found the perfect dress for you," Liz yelled from another rack. She held up a hanger with a dress on it. I took it from her and looked at it. It was sapphire blue, and it was beautiful. I tried it on to make sure it fit, and it did.

A-line form fit against my figure, as it fell to my knees. It was perfect. I changed back into my clothes, then found matching shoes. I didn't hesitate to plunk down cash onto the counter to buy it. Yes, it was seventy dollars, but it was well worth it.

After getting my change, I grabbed my shopping bags, and we made our way home. I'm excited to be going to Homecoming, even if it was with Jonas Gray.

The week flew by, and before I knew it, Homecoming finally arrived. I got dressed, fixing my hair and makeup. Jonas would be here soon because Lucille would make sure of it.

While I was getting ready, so was Jonas.

"Big date?" Nate asked him.

"Tonight is Patty's Homecoming," he said, pulling on a dress shoe. "So, I'm getting ready to go pick her up."

Nate furrowed his eyebrows at him. "So, this like some date?"

"Nope, two friends going to a school dance," he said as he finished tying his other shoe and standing up. He grabbed his suit coat and pulled it on, then checked himself in the mirror.

"Does she know that?" Nate questioned him.

"Yeah, why?"

"Cause some girls to get the wrong idea, you know?" Jonas could hear the tension in Nate's voice.

Choosing to ignore it, he said, "Are you sure it's not you getting the wrong idea?"

"Why would I get the wrong idea?" It filled his question with irritation.

"Because I'm getting the third degree," he said, walking over to him. "Look, we're going to the dance tonight as two friends. But then again, I have that Gray charm so, anything is possible," he smirked.

Nate gazed at him as Jonas remarked, "Or unless you can decide and do something about it."

"I don't know what you're talking about?" Nate lied to him.

"Uh-huh, sure, you don't. Keep denying what's in front of you. One day, you'll deny how you feel," he said, walking past him to collect my corsage.

Jonas walked into the kitchen. Lucille checked him out, making sure everything looked good.

"Well," she asked him.

"Oh, he's got it bad. He's too stubborn to admit it," Jonas whispered as she pinned his boutonniere to his lapel.

"Don't worry. I have a feeling there is a reason Nate's waiting." She winked at him.

Jonas grabbed the plastic package and walked out of the door. He walked across the street to collect me and bring me back so he could drive us to the dance. Plus, he wanted Nate to get a fantastic view of what I looked like in my dress.

I answered the door and spoke to Jonas. I yelled to my parents; I left for the dance and walked out, following Jonas back to his car. As we walked onto the driveway, Lucille greeted us, taking a million pictures, oh Lucille.

Nate opened the door to the garage from the house and looked in our direction.

"She's beautiful, isn't she?" Cayson asked, standing next to him. Nate looked at him then back at us. Something was boiling inside of him, seeing me with Jonas. A feeling he hated more than anything, jealousy.

Jonas and I got into the car, and he looked at me. "Should we go have some fun?"

"Yes, we should," I smiled back at him. He started the car and pulled out of the driveway, heading to the Homecoming dance.

He pulled into the parking lot, and like a gentleman, he opened my door and held out his arm. Lucille would wring his neck if he didn't.

We walked into the school, and the music was playing with people dancing. We made our way to the dance floor and started dancing. I had to admit that Jonas was a superb dancer. We danced fast and slow, taking a break to get some refreshments.

"Patty!" Liz squealed. She hugged me and introduced me to her date, Keith. She looked at Jonas. "Wow, you, Gray, boys clean up."

"We try," he grinned, and I laughed. Jonas was the easygoing one out of all the brothers. He had that likable personality.

"I don't know about you girls, but this is supposed to be a dance, so let's dance," he suggested.

The four of us walked back onto the dance floor and danced. When a slow song came on, he danced with me, and we talked.

"You know Nate couldn't take his eyes off of you this evening."

"Oh?" I asked him, confused.

"Yep," he said, spinning me than bringing me back, "he'll never admit it, but he likes you."

"He does. I'm like a little sister to him," I sighed, rolling my eyes.

"Yeah, but the way he looks at you is not how Cayson and I look at you."

"What do you mean?"

"I mean, he doesn't look at you as a little sister," he said as he twirled me again. We danced and didn't talk about Nate anymore after that. I couldn't help but think about what he said.

When the dance ended, he drove me home. My thoughts kept running about what Jonas said at the dance. Nate? Likes me more than like a sister? I didn't know how to feel about that. I always had a crush on Nate growing up, but it had diminished as I aged.

He pulled into my driveway, and I got out of the car. He backed out of my driveway and went over to his house. I walked up the front steps, went inside, entered my room, and turned on the light. I set my clutch down and pulled a clip out of my hair, holding in place.

I walked over to the window that faced the backyard. I went to draw the shades, then something caught my eye, or should I say, someone, Nate.

He was sitting on the top of the picnic table out in the back. I walked out of my room, through the kitchen, and to the back door. I opened it and stepped outside over to him.

"Nate?"

"Hey, Patty," he answered.

"What are you doing here?"

He climbed off the picnic table and walked over to me. "I didn't have time to tell you how beautiful you looked tonight."

"Wait, you waited until I got home to tell me I looked beautiful?"

"Better late than never, right?"

I smiled at him, and he shrugged.

"Do you think I could have a dance?" He asked me.

"There's no music," I reminded him.

"Hold on," he pulled a tape player out of his pocket and placed it on the table, then hit play. A song started playing. "Okay, now can I have a dance?"

"Sure," I answered.

I reached up, placing a hand on his shoulder and my other side in his as he put his other hand on the lower part of my back. He started dancing with me then pulled me close. I leaned my head on his chest as he held me close.

We didn't talk but danced, and it was lovely. Being close to Nate, I could smell his cologne. It was intoxicating. I could not get enough of that smell. We danced, and he was gentle when he held me. As the song played and we danced, I couldn't help but remember what Jonas said.

I felt something deep inside of me; I never thought it was possible. I liked Nate, and it was more than as a friend, oh dear.

We finished our dance, and he bid me goodnight, and I went back inside. I walked into the house, making my way to my room. As I went to close the blinds, I saw him linger then smile before turning and walking away.

It was the best Homecoming ever.

CHAPTER 11

APPLE ORCHARD FUN

"Yo, Peppermint Patty, you coming or what?" Jonas yelled through my window.

I opened my screen and stuck my head out the window. "Where?"

"To the apple orchard," he grinned. I looked to see his brothers, my brother, and Liz standing out in the back.

"It's Sunday," I grumbled.

"Yeah, and your point?" Cayson questioned me.

"Sunday is to be a day of rest. So, that means I take a nap. You guys have fun." I waved at them, shutting my screen along with my window.

I needed a nap. This entire thing about getting up early for school was utter bullshit. Who does that? I would be so glad when I graduated, and I was taking afternoon classes.

I lay on my bed and got comfy when I heard a knock at the door. "Go away, Danny!"

They knocked again as the door opened up, then I picked up a shoe and threw it at them. Nate ducked, causing the sneaker to fly past him and land in the hallway.

I stared at him. "I thought you were Danny."

"Nah, he's shorter and thinner than me," he smirked.

"I'm not going. I'm taking a nap."

"Fine," he shrugged.

I laid back down and closed my eyes until I felt someone grab me, picking me up. I opened my eyes only to come face to face with Nate's butt.

"Nate!"

"You can sleep, but you're still going," he said as a matter of fact.

I looked at his butt, and I had to admit; he had a nice butt. Why fight it? I'll admire the view from here, sigh.

He carried me outside and tossed me into his car. Danny handed me a pair of shoes, and Liz gave me a hoodie. Those sneaky sneaks. They planned this.

Nate got into the car, pulling out of the driveway, and the six of us went to the apple orchard.

It didn't take long to get to the orchard. It was cold enough for a hoodie with the crisp, chilly October air, without having to get our parkas out. Michigan weather in the winter is a bitch. It's freezing because it surrounds us by four Great Lakes. Yes, we have five, but one doesn't even touch us.

I was thankful it was at least sunny out. Usually, we have grey skies that are the chance of rain or snow.

We got out of the car and walked into the building. Danny paid for a bushel of apples, and they handed him a bag. Mom wants a particular apple called Ida Reds for pies. The thought of Mom's homemade apple pie baking in the oven made my mouth water.

We walked around the orchard, making our way to Ida Red trees, and started picking. We had to climb the trees to get to the best apples. They post signs not to climb the trees. We didn't listen; we never do.

"Yo, Nate, hold that bag, will ya?" Danny yelled down to him. He picked up the bag and held it open as we threw apples at him. He caught them with the kit.

When we figured we had enough, we climbed down out of the tree.

"You two are something else," he chuckled, shaking his head.

"At least I'm better at climbing trees than I was when I was younger," I grinned, making him laugh even more.

"Donuts?" Danny asked us.

"Definitely," I added.

We walked back to the building and got some warm donuts with cinnamon and icy apple cider. It was always a treat when you went to the orchard.

We sat at the table, munching on the deliciousness called donuts when nature called. Man cider goes through you.

I came out of the bathroom when I ran smack into Brian Holloway great.

"Aww, look what we have here," he smirked. His buddies chuckled.

"I don't see your bodyguards around," he said as a matter of fact.

I looked at him, "Oh, they're here, and so is my brother," I couldn't help the icy-ness of my tone.

"Well, I guess we can have some fun before they realize you're in trouble," he said with a tone full of hate. "Grab Patty," he ordered them, and they grabbed me.

Oh, hell, no, I know where this is going. So, I did what any smart girl would do. I screamed, "Fire!"

That causes people to stop and stare.

"Shut her up," Brian growled.

One of them covered my mouth, so I bit him, "Ow! She bit me!" He shook his hand.

"Fine, let me handle this," he said as he stood in front of me and pulled back his fist. I closed my eyes, but the fist never connected with my face.

I opened my eyes to see Nate holding Brian's fist.

"Yeah, I don't think so. I warned you," Nate said as he hauled off and hit Brian.

"Drop her," my brother ordered, and they let go of me. He threw a punch at both of them, connecting with their faces. Damn! My brother can hit.

Nate leaned down and grabbed Brian by the hoodie, lifting him off the ground. "Leave her alone. Period," he growled. Was it wrong that I found that hot?

Brian rubbed his jaw and got up, stumbling away with his buddies following behind. Nate walked over to Danny and me, "How is it that you going to the bathroom by yourself gets you into trouble?"

"Pure dumb luck, I guess," I shrugged, causing him to chuckle.

"Has anyone seen the other three stooges," Danny asked us, and we shook our head. He was right. Where the heck were they?

"Okay, so we know they like each other from what happened Homecoming night. The question remains, how do we get them together?" Cayson asked Jonas and Liz.

"Well, Nate won't touch her until she turns eighteen," Jonas told him.

"Why not?" Cayson asked him.

"Don't want to go to jail," he shrugged.

"Okay, so when does she turn eighteen?"

"How the hell should I know?" Jonas said.

"November 15," Liz interjected.

"What?" They both asked her.

"She turns eighteen November 15 this year. She has a birthday coming up. Didn't you guys know that?" She looked at both of them, and they both shrugged. "Wait, you have known this girl your entire life, and you don't even know when her birthday is? You're pathetic."

"Well, it's not like we keep track of these things," Cayson said with an eye roll.

She shook her head and rolled her eyes. "Look, if you want to get them together, she turns eighteen on November 15." She smirked and turned around, walking away.

"Okay, November 15 is the big day," Jonas said to Cayson.

"Yeah, the day he declares his undying love for her and ma gets off our back," Cayson reminded him.

"That'll never happen."

"Don't kill my dreams, man," Cayson countered.

"The only dream you should have would work at a job, like the rest of us adults," he shot back at him.

Cayson sighed and shook his head. "I start tomorrow."

"That's what you said last week."

"Well, is it my fault they screwed up my paperwork? No," Cayson told him as he walked away from Jonas.

"Likely story!" He yelled to Cayson, flipped him off. Such brother loves with the Gray boys.

We waited for them to come back when Liz walked over and sat down next to Danny.

"Where were you guys?" I asked her.

"Tweedledee and Tweedledum couldn't find the Ida Red section. Even though there are signs posted everywhere," she said with an eye roll.

"Sounds about right," Nate chuckled.

"So, Danny, isn't Patty's birthday coming up?" She inquired to my brother.

"Huh?" She elbowed him. "Oh, right, yes, yes, her birthday is coming up."

I looked up at them. What the hell are they babbling about at the table?

Nate leaned away and rubbed his chin. "You have a birthday coming up?"

"Yeah, so?"

"So, that means you turned the big 1-8, right?" Danny asked me.

I gave him a weird look. "You should know this, considering we live in the same house."

"I'm saying."

"That you don't know how old I am? Dude, we're three and a half years apart to the day," I said to him. Okay, Liz was acting weirder than usual, and my brother was acting even stranger. Who the hell forgets their own siblings' birthday and age?

"So, will there be a party with food, cake, and all that good junk?" Nate asked me as he sat with his chin in his hand.

"Mom hasn't talked to me about it. Why?" I asked.

"Because if there is cake, my brothers and I love cake. We love to eat as much cake as possible," he mentioned to me. What the hell is wrong with everyone, and why is cake so damn important?

"Ooh, cake, the cake is great, especially when it gets on your lips and make them look so delectable," Liz chimed in.

"I'm sure if there is cake, there are napkins," I reminded them.

"Yeah, but sometimes one needs help to clean off the frosting from one's lips," Danny added. Okay, this conversation was getting weirder by the minute.

"Okay, I don't know what is wrong with you guys, but cake isn't such a brilliant idea," I said, giving them a weird look.

"Oh no, you have a cake for your birthday. It's a tradition," Nate said, wiggling his eyebrows and smiling at me.

"I'm over this entire cake conversation. It's making me not want any," I said, getting up and walking away.

"That was a little weird," Danny said to them.

"Don't worry, I have a feeling there is cake," Nate smirked as he got up from the table and followed behind me.

"Did I miss something?" Danny questioned Liz.

Liz patted his shoulder. "More than you know." She got up, leaving him sitting there, dumbfounded.

CHAPTER 12

HALLOWEEN, TRICK OR TREATING, AND SCARY MOVIES

With the weirdness going around, it wasn't surprising that it had to do with Halloween coming up. At least, I don't think it did. The Gray boys were acting stranger than usual, but they're always strange. My brother was acting weird, and Liz was acting odd.

I swear this world is weird, and I live in it.

I tried to ignore it and focus on fun, like Halloween. Since this was my last year in high school, I went trick or treating. Don't judge. It's free candy, man, plus, we get to dress up.

Since Liz harped on me going to Homecoming, I harped on her to trick or to treat.

"This is dumb. Why can't we go to a Halloween party?" She whined. I rolled my eyes as I finished getting ready.

"Stop complaining. We get free candy and get to dress up. Plus, I don't feel too bad because I'm not eighteen yet," I said, turning to her and smiling.

"Fine, let's get this over with," she groaned.

"Why? Do you have a recent date or something?" I asked her.

"No!" she responded. I gave her a look. She is acting weird. Oh well, time for candy.

We went out to trick or treat. We had to go to the next street over because very few people handed out candy on my street — damn Scrooge's.

Each house we went to, we knocked, yelled trick, or treat. We got looks along with some candy thrown into our pillowcases. Even though Liz complained at first, she had fun.

We finished up and made our way back to my house. It was already dark, and most people were turning off their porch lights. Trick or treating's over. Well, until I had kids and could go again.

As we walked home, I got the feeling someone was following us. An icy shiver ran down my spine, so I picked up the pace. The only problem was that the people did too until we were running for my house.

Then it happened. Someone jumped out in a mask, yelling, "Rawr," causing us to scream. Hearing laughter, I stopped and looked at them.

"Oh, that was classic," they said under the mask. What in the hell? They were laughing and clapping their hands. I walked over and pulled up their cover, Cayson.

I should have known. Then we heard more laughing. We turned to see Nate, Jonas, and Danny stepping out from the shadows, rolling with laughter. I narrowed my lips and glared at them.

"Real cute, you guys," I huffed.

"We thought so," Danny laughed.

"Why?" I looked at him.

"Because you scare and its Halloween," he grinned. I smacked him.

"How did you find us?" I inquired.

"We were walking around and saw the two of you heading for home. Plus, Mom wanted to make sure you both were okay," he shrugged.

I shook my head and rolled my eyes. I was almost eighteen. I'm sure I can take care of myself.

"We're going back to the Gray house to watch horror films if you both want to join us," Danny suggested to Liz and me.

Before I responded, Liz said, "Sure." I looked at her, and she winked at me. I never understand my best friend. But then again, she is a teenage girl.

I sighed, and we all walked back to the Gray house to watch movies. It's an enjoyable thing that I had on a comfy costume since I didn't go home and change, or I would be so screwed right now.

We walked into their house and made our way to the family room. Cayson popped in a movie then settled in, as did the rest of us. Liz and I sat on the loveseat while Jonas and Nate sat on the couch, and my brother and Cayson sat on the floor. Now pay close attention to our seating arrangements.

The girls are on the loveseat. The two older Gray boys are on the other couch, got it? Cayson and Danny are on the floor, okay? Now that we're clear on that, this is when musical seats happened.

The movie engrossed me so much that I didn't notice they all switched spots. Liz got up from next to me with Nate taking her place. She sat next to Danny, taking Cayson's seat, and Cayson moved next to Jonas, taking Nate's place.

Halfway through the film, a scary scene hit. I screamed and jumped in my seat, only pulled close to someone. Why the hell is Liz holding me? I turned to ask her when I noticed she was next to Danny, and Cayson was next to Jonas. My eyes widened, and I turned to see Nate holding me with a smile.

My heart started beating through my chest. I swear the entire neighborhood heard it. I gulped hard and said, "Uh." Yeah, no words were forming, and I was nervous.

"Yes," he asked me in a whisper. His voice is silky as I stared at him wide-eyed. I had sat next to Nate before. I have touched him back, you know, helping him up, but never in my life have I ever been in this proximity to him. It made me nervous.

He leaned close to my face, and I felt his fiery breath fan my cheek. He made his way to my ear and whispered, "I want to kiss you, but one, your brother is here, and so are mine; two, you're not eighteen."

He moved back from me, and I pushed his arms off me. He smirked, and I gazed at him. At that moment, I didn't know what to think. Was this a game to him? I didn't know, and I didn't want to find out.

I got up from my seat and moved to a recliner, leaving him confused. Good, because he made me confused.

"How come you're sitting over there?" Danny asked me.

"Because I wanted to get comfortable," I shot back and shooting a glare at Nate. Sometimes my brother was clueless.

We finished watching some movies, and as soon as the last film ended, I snatched up my candy and stormed home. I would not be some game to anyone, no matter what.

"What's up with Patty?" Jonas asked Nate.

"Beats me." Nate shrugged, walking to his room.

"Big brother has blown it," Cayson said.

"Blown what?" Danny asked.

"Danny, walk me home. I'll explain this minor thing called liking someone," Liz said. She grabbed his arm and led him out of Gray's house.

Jonas looked at Cayson. "All this work, and he blows it in a matter of seconds. Ma will kill us."

Cayson thought about it, tapping his finger against these lips then snapping them. "I got it. I know how we can get those two finally together."

"How?"

"We still have the cabin up north, right?"

"Yeah, so?"

"So, we need our mothers to send them on a brief road trip together and alone," Cayson grinned.

"I doubt that happens," Jonas remarked.

"You doubt ma's deceitful behavior?" Cayson looked at him.

"No, that I don't doubt, but I doubt they would both agree to it," he said to Cayson.

"Well, that's why we leave that part up to me," Cayson responded with a shrug.

"Yeah, but when?"

"Hunting season is coming up, so we can have her persuade them to get the cabin ready for Dad and our uncles," Cayson said.

"I'm beginning to wonder if you didn't get more of ma's genes than our dad's," Jonas commented to him.

"I'm happy about that because our dad, well, he is scary," he remarked to Jonas.

"I'll never understand what the problem is with Nate, you, and dad."

"It's simple; Nate is like dad, and dad thinks I'm a screw-up," he shrugged, walking away.

Did he want to kiss me? But I didn't because my brother was there and I wasn't eighteen! Unbelievable!

I paced back and forth in my room, mumbling to myself in frustration. One minute, people tell me Nate likes me, which is weird, then said he wants to kiss me but doesn't.

One minute he acts like I'm a pain in the ass, and the next, he's all flirty. Hot and cold, hot and cold, I tell you! Why can't a guy be like, hey, I like you? Do you want me? Let's go out. Is it that complicated?

I sat down on my bed in a huff. Why is it every time I like a guy, they either make my life miserable or give me mixed signals? And people wonder why I don't date. Perfect example right there.

I'll focus on school and work. I know those were two constants in my life I could count on. I didn't have to deal with the emotional rollercoasters of liking someone that comes with it.

Guys were confusing.

CHAPTER 13

PARTY ISSUES

I decided after Halloween to keep my distance from the Gray boys. It seemed like I had nothing but issues every time I was around them. Plus, I wanted to focus on school and work.

Liz had other ideas like the party she decided we should attend Friday night. I didn't know about this plan. All I knew was I would stay the night, and we had a girl's night. That comprises junk food, movies, and gossip.

The only thing was that she had other ideas. Why do I have a terrible feeling about this?

As we walked to someone's house whom I didn't know, all I could think of was this was a terrible idea.

"Come on, Patty!" She yelled at me.

I walked a little behind her with my arms crossed. "Liz, why are we going to a party? If our parents find out," I said.

She stopped and turned to me. "They won't find out. Live a little, Patty." I looked at her as my stomach churned. I didn't like this idea one bit. I wasn't the girl to do things behind her parent's back. I didn't get into trouble. I was responsible and followed the rules.

Liz did things that went against the rules, which made her a rule breaker. We were the opposites. How we were best friends were beyond me? But we were.

I took a deep breath as I followed her to a house. You could hear the music five houses down because it was loud. We walked up to find people hanging outside, some were entering, and some were leaving. But the one thing they all had, a cup in their hand, which I'm sure was alcohol-related.

We walked in, and a few people greeted her, handing her a cup. She smiled and took it, drinking from it like it was water. They gave me a cup, but I declined it. You never know what they might slip in it.

I looked around and saw that it was most of the people from school here. The problem was I didn't know most of them.

I tried to stick close to Liz, but she disappeared off somewhere, leaving me to fend for myself, great.

I walked around. People were talking and dancing. Some were playing drinking games. Some were making out. Gross. It was a typical teenage party.

I found myself in the kitchen and noticed a punch bowl. At least they have the punch to drink. Not thinking, I picked up a glass and filled it to the rim. I took a sip. What was the heck of a kind of drink is this?

I made a face but figured it was an off-brand. Shrugging, I drank. At some point, I don't know if it was after the second cup or fourth that I was feeling good. I also developed an insane amount of courage to the point. I danced a lot.

Taking a break, I stumbled around and came across a phone. Oh goody, I call Nate and give him a piece of my mind. I mean, why not? Someone should put him in his place to lead a girl on and playing games.

I picked up the receiver and tried to focus on the numbers. It was a little challenging when there were two phones. Who has two phones side by side? Isn't one enough? Eh must have teens in the house.

After I hit the last number, it rang. It took twice until someone picked up.

"Hello?" Their voice answered, and I had a hard time understanding who it was.

"Nate?"

"No, it's Jonas."

"Oh, hey Jonas," I said.

"Patty? Where are you, and why is there loud music?" He asked me as I swayed back and forth.

"I am at a party, and where I am is none of your business, because well, I don't know where I am," I said, slurring my words.

"Tell me the address. I'll come and get you," Jonas offered.

"Nope," I slurred, popping the p. "I want to speak to Nate. Then I never bother you again."

"Are you drunk?"

"Nah, all I drank was some punch. Punch doesn't make you drunken. Now go get Nate," I slurred, swaying back and forth. I placed a hand on the wall, trying to steady myself.

The next thing I heard was a distinct voice. "Patty?"

"Nate?"

"Yeah," he answered.

"I have a bone to pick with you, mister hot and cold, who refuses to kiss me because he's dumb," I slurred my words.

"Are you drunk?" It filled his tone of concern.

"Nope, I had punch."

"Where are you?"

"I don't know, but that's not why I'm calling you. I'm calling you to tell you don't have to worry anymore about me. You made yourself loud and clear. You don't want me, which is fine because I won't bother you anymore even though I like you. I've moved on from you," I said, trying to steady myself.

"I'm coming to get you," he said to me.

"Nope, no need, you don't care about me, and that's fine because I have a house full of many people that care about me."

"Patty, I'm getting dressed and coming to get you. Now tell me where you are," he growled.

"You're sexy when you growl," I giggled. Then I heard Nate sigh. "But I'm good. Got to go. I need some punch. Ta ta," I said as I dropped the receiver and staggered away as he yelled my name into it. Someone walked by and hung it up.

I walked over to the punch bowl and refilled my cup. Whatever type of punch this was, it was outstanding.

I didn't have a care in the world as I drank and stumbled around. It felt good telling Nate off because I didn't need him. I didn't need anyone; I was my person.

As I made my way around, I didn't know I had a company show up in the Gray boys' form.

"All right, split up and find her," Nate ordered Jonas and Cayson. They nodded, and each searched a part of the house for me.

At one point, Nate found me. I was staggering and swaying as I tried to walk; he walked over and spun me around.

"Nate! What are you doing here?" I exclaimed, trying to keep my balance.

"I'm taking you home," he replied in a firm tone.

"But I'm staying with Liz, who is somewhere here. I don't know where. She's making out with some boy," I giggled.

"Not tonight. I'm taking you back to my house."

"Stop!" I held out my hand, placing it on his chest. "Are you trying to seduce me? Because it won't work. You won't even kiss me."

"You know why I won't kiss you," he responded.

"Yep, because I'm Patty. Kid sister to Danny. Neighbor obedient girl, who gets harassed by her crush. Then gets played by her neighbor," I said, giggling.

"I already told you why," he reminded me.

"But that's not the actual reason. But it's all good," I said, waving my arms around. "I'm used to being second fiddle. I mean, I'm not the girl guys like you go after, right? I am too nice."

He stood there as I continued my drunken rant.

"But let me tell you something. I may be a likable girl, but I'm also one of a kind." I turned and walked away from him, dropping my cup into a garbage can. "Patty has left the building!"

Jonas and Cayson found Nate as he said, "Found Patty."

"And?" Jonas asked him.

"She's drunk, very drunk," he sighed.

Liz walked up to them. "What are you guys doing here?"

"We should ask you the same thing?" Nate said, looking at her, annoyed.

"Patty and I came to a party."

"Oh yeah? Because coming to a party with your best friend means ditching them. They can get drunk off their ass," he remarked to her.

"But she took nothing to drink from anyone," she said.

"Well, she got it from somewhere. So, I do what any best friend would do and take care of her. You need to rethink what your friendship means to her," he snapped as he walked away. Jonas and Cayson followed him.

They found me halfway down the street as I stumbled to walk home. I wasn't feeling good, and everything was spinning. The next thing I knew, I stumbled onto the grass and heaved.

I felt my hair pulled away from my face as someone rubbed my back. I fell to my knees and continued to heave until there was nothing left.

I sat down, and Jonas handed Nate a napkin to clean my face off. I stared at Nate as he wiped off my mouth and chin. Once he finished cleaning me up, he helped me up. I looked at him until I passed out, with him catching me in his arms. I'm tired.

He picked me up bridal style, carried me to his car, set me in the back seat, and then closed the door. I couldn't tell you what happened after that because I was out cold. All I knew was that I was never drinking again, ever.

CHAPTER 14

AFTER PARTY ISSUES

Nate pulled in and got out of the car. He pulled me out and placed me over his shoulder. I was out for the count. Guess alcohol and heaving do that to you.

They went around back and carried me inside, met by Lucille.

"Do I want to know?" she asked them.

"Let's say that Patty and alcohol don't mix," Cayson said.

"Ma, would you think you can cover for her?" Nate asked her.

She gave them a look. "Look, whom you're talking to."

"Yeah, I know," Nate reminded her.

"Yes, now put her in your room. I'll phone Joan letting her know that Patty got sick. I had you pick her up because we didn't want to disturb her house so late," she spoke.

He carried me to his room, laying me down on his bed. I started mumbling something in my sleep. He leaned down and took a listen.

"Nate's a wonderful guy; I wish he liked me as much as I liked him," I whispered as he heard soft snores follow afterward.

He leaned into my ear and whispered, "More than you know."

He covered me up and walked out of the room, closing the door behind him. He stood in the hallway and smiled.

I woke up, groaning. My head felt like it would explode. I sat up and rubbed my eyes, looking around the room. How the hell did I get here, and where was I?

After getting my eyes to focus, I looked around; then I saw them, model cars. The only one I knew whom model cars had was, oh, shit. I stood up and looked around.

The last thing I remember was walking into a house with Liz and losing Liz in said house. I looked down and saw the clothes I had on last night, oh, well.

While I was losing my mind, my bladder decided it needed emptying. I flung the door open and ran to the bathroom.

"Patty's up," Jonas smirked while eating breakfast.

A few minutes later, I came out of the bathroom and walked down the hallway to the kitchen. Sitting at the table was Nate, Jonas, and Cayson, eating breakfast. Lucille was making a cup of coffee.

"Morning drunk," Cayson snickered.

I looked at them and wanted to crawl in a hole, dying at that precise moment. Lucille handed me a glass of water and two aspirins. I swallowed them.

Then she handed me a cup of black coffee. I took it from her and walked over, taking a seat between Jonas and Cayson.

"So, what exactly happened last night?" I asked them.

"You mean you don't remember?" Nate asked me as he ate his breakfast, not bothering to look at me.

"No, I remember going to some party with Liz," I tried to recall, but after that, everything was hazy.

"Let me refresh your memory. You went to this party and got drunk on a spiked punch. Then you drunken dialed me, telling me you were over me and didn't need me to care about you. When I showed up, you told me you had feelings for me, then walked away. That was all before you puked in someone's yard," he answered as he gave me a stern look.

I stared at him, horrified.

"But, that's okay, they say there are two types of honest people. Kids and drunk people," he replied while not looking at me but kept eating. I didn't know what to say. I felt mortified and like shit.

Jonas and Cayson said nothing, and neither did Lucille. I felt like a pariah right now. You say nasty things to someone you like when your drunk doesn't go over well with their family.

I got up and whispered, "Excuse me." Then walked out of the kitchen to the front door. I opened it, stepped out onto the porch, closing it behind me, and going home. I knew going to that party was a disaster in the making.

I walked into my house and went straight to my bedroom. I kicked off my shoes and crawled into bed, pulling the covers over my head. If I had a chance with Nate last night, I blew it. I am never drinking again.

I stayed in bed all day, only getting up to use the bathroom, here and there. I didn't want to talk to anyone. I humiliated myself. I gained liquid courage and told a guy I was developing feelings for, off.

That night, I lay in bed and watched TV. I ate nothing because my stomach was still woozy from the night before.

I knew I would have to face everyone, but not right now.

The next day, I finally came out of my bedroom and took a shower. I needed it. I didn't shower yesterday, and I wanted to wash away the whole situation.

After I finished, I turned the shower off and got out. I dried off and wrapped a towel around me. I wiped off the mirror and looked at my reflection. Even if Nate became interested in me, why would he? I mean, Friday night proved how immature I was. He was twenty-four, and I was seventeen. I sighed.

I went into my room and put on some dry, comfy clothes. I walked out and went into the kitchen, taking a seat at the table.

"How are you feeling? Lucille said you got sick Friday," Mom said to me.

I shrugged. "Okay."

She made me something to eat.

"So, your birthday is next week. Do you know what you wanted to do?" She asked me.

"I was thinking of staying in and watching movies," I mentioned to her.

"You don't want a party?" I could hear the disappointment in her voice with her question. Mom enjoyed celebrating our birthdays. I couldn't stop her from that. She gave us life.

"I guess a small get-together would be fine," I suggested offering a slight smile. Even though I felt like dirt, I couldn't ruin Mom's enthusiasm to celebrate my birth.

I knew one thing was for sure Nate wouldn't be there. He must hate me. Scratch that, I know he hates me.

All week I went to school and worked. Liz and I talked after I scolded her for abandoning me. Like most friends, we made up. I also told her what happened with Nate and what I said. I didn't need her pity. It was my doing.

While I kept myself busy, everyone else was planning a surprise of their own for me.

Lucille hung up the phone and looked at her boys. "It's all set. She doesn't suspect a thing." A smile curled upon her lips.

"This birthday is one she'll never forget," Cayson grinned.

"Now, this is what we do," she said to them as she explained what would happen. Yep, Lucille was plotting and planning as usual.

As my birthday drew near, I was getting anxious. Here I was turning eighteen and never had a boyfriend or a kiss. Mom said I was a late bloomer, but I wanted to wait for that right guy. I thought it was Brian Holloway, but that never happened.

Mom invited a few people over, which was beautiful, and she made me a chocolate cake since it was my favorite.

I stood at my window and looked out of it at the picnic table. I thought about the nights Nate and I would talk. I miss those talks.

Seeing it sit empty, surrounded by almost bare trees and grey skies, bummed me out. I sighed. Whatever I thought was happening between Nate and me was a fleeting moment. The thought depressed me.

Well, Happy Birthday to me.

CHAPTER 15

HAPPY 18 BIRTHDAY, PATTY!

My family woke me yelling, "Happy Birthday!" They realize I have a school, right?

I groaned and threw a shoe at them.

"Yep, I'm not a morning person," Danny commented on my lack of cheery personality in the morning.

I looked at the clock. It's at five a.m. Is my family insane? I rolled back over until my alarm went off.

It felt like I closed my eyes when my alarm started blaring—going to school on your birthday sucks. Why couldn't I have a birthday where I didn't have a school? Thanks, Mom and Dad, for having me in November.

I got up and dressed, so I could eat before going to school. Let's hope today doesn't suck.

Today didn't suck like I thought it would. Liz was walking home with me to celebrate my birthday. Mom invited a few people over for pizza and cake.

Lucille, Jonas, and Cayson came along with my family and a few others. I greeted them at the door. I looked to see if Nate was coming, but he wasn't. That made me feel a little down, but I hid it.

Lucille handed me a bag, and they wished me a happy birthday. Well, at least they came.

All evening I talked to people, had a pizza, cake, and opened gifts. It was a sweet birthday, considering my disappointment.

I was in the kitchen, getting ready to refill my drink when I felt someone stand behind me. I turned, and there Nate was.

"Happy birthday, Patty," Nate said to me.

My eyes widened. "Thanks."

He walked closer to me as I leaned with my back into the counter. His face was inches from mine as he placed his hands on the countertop on each side of me.

He leaned into me. "Remember when I said I wanted to kiss you?"

"Yeah?" My breathing hitched.

"I also said I wanted to wait until you were eighteen, and today you turned eighteen," he reminded me.

My eyes flicked from his eyes to his lips. I never realized how full they looked up close and personal. I could feel my heart beating out of my chest as I swallowed hard.

"Now, I'll kiss you," he said to me.

My lips parted when he said that. Oh, god, he moved one hand to my hip and then placed his other hand on my face. He took his thumb and traced it over my bottom lip, sending shivers down my back.

I thought he would lean in and kiss me, he pulled back, leaving me confused.

"Kidding," he smirked.

What happened?

When I realized what he did, my face turned to horror, so I did what I do well. I let my anger get the best of me. I grabbed some chocolate cake and shoved it in his face, taking him by surprise.

As I held the remnants of chocolate cake in my hand, and he yelled, "What was that for?"

"You shouldn't have teased me," I spat.

I could see the anger boiling inside of him, and before I knew it, he grabbed me. I squirmed. "Let me go!"

"No! Not before I do this!" he barked.

Oh, dear god, what's he going to do?

He grabbed my face and crashed his lips into mine, taking me by surprise. I fought at first but then gave in and kissed him back.

I moved my arms around the back of his neck and wrapped his arms around my waist. He licked my lips with his tongue, wanting entrance, and I opened my mouth to give it to him. Our tongues swirled around each other as he deepened the kiss.

It was by far the best first kiss I ever had. It was everything I had hoped for in an embrace. It was passionate and exhilarating. At that moment, I knew my feelings for Nate went deeper than some childhood crush.

He pulled back as we stood there, catching our breath. I looked at him, and he looked at me; saying nothing, he leaned in and kissed me again. This time it was sweet.

After playing tonsil hockey, even though I had mine removed at three, he finally released my lips, but he didn't release me. He kept a firm hold on me.

I was speechless.

"I guess this changes things, doesn't it?" He asked me in an indistinct voice.

"Do you want it to change things?" I asked wide-eyed, hoping he would say yes. Please say yes.

"You do not understand how much I want this to change things," he responded to me.

My lips curled upwards until I was grinning. "Oh?"

"Yes," he smirked as he said that, "but we'll take this slow."

"What do you mean?" My brows moved into a look of confusion.

"Let's start with a date. Patty, I want to do things right with you because if I screw this up, my ma will kill me."

I couldn't help but giggle. Lucille would kill him if he messed this up.

I pulled away from him, confusing him, and turned to the kitchen sink. I grabbed a washcloth and wet it. I turned back around as I started cleaning off his face, and everywhere else, there was chocolate cake.

He smiled, as did I, while I cleaned him up. Then when I finished, he reached out and pulled me close to him. "I thought you wanted to take this slow?" I asked him.

"I do, but I also enjoy being close to you," he smirked. I rolled my eyes at him.

"Okay, Romeo, but I have a party to get back to," I said. I pulled away and walked back into the living room. He caught my hand and slid his into mine, intertwining our fingers. I couldn't help but smile at how weird but wondrous this felt.

We were about to walk hand in hand into the party, I stopped.

"What?" He looked at me, confused.

"I came in here to get a drink, but your lips distracted me." He chuckled, and I went over to pour a cup of pop. Then I stopped when it hit me, all those things I said to him. Now, I felt like a fool.

"Patty?"

I turned to him and gave him a look which caused him concerned.

"What is it?" He asked me.

"That night, I said some horrible things to you, even though I don't remember them," I sighed.

He walked over to me. "Yes, you did, but you also said something that put things in perspective."

"What was that?"

"You wanted me to like you as much as you liked me," he told me.

I looked at him, and he reached up, tucking a strand of hair behind my ear.

"I figured you were honest with your feelings when you said those things to me. It was a defense mechanism for you. After what Brian put you through, you didn't want to get close. You wouldn't get your heart broke, so you did what any girl would do and try to push me away."

"I feel horrible about it." I did. I felt terrible about it. Nate and I may have had our difficulties, but he has always been there for me.

"I know, and I plan on reminding you the rest of your life about it," he smirked as he turned and walked away.

Jerk.

I rolled my eyes and picked up my cup as I followed behind him into the living room. I went to sit down. He grabbed me and pulled me onto his lap. He wrapped his arms around my waist and nuzzled his head into the crook of my neck.

"Nate, people will see us," I whispered.

"So, let them." I couldn't help but smile.

Even if everyone noticed, they said nothing, which I was glad. The last thing I needed was some stupid joke about this. I couldn't help but feel like this was a temporary thing that tomorrow I would wake up, and it would be a dream.

Then I felt soft lips press against the back of my neck. Hell, if this is a dream, I never want to wake up.

Everyone pretty much left around ten, and the only two people left were Nate and me. He stayed to help me clean up.

"So, about that date?"

I looked at him.

"I was thinking this Friday, dinner, and a movie? You know something traditional."

"Dinner and a movie sound good," I said.

"Good," he said to me.

"You know, that kiss in the kitchen, well, that was my first kiss," I said.

"I know."

I stopped. "You knew?"

"Yeah, Danny mentioned it, plus you never dated before," he reminded me.

"Oh," I said.

"Every girl deserves a first kiss that leaves her toes curled and her mind blown," he said. He tossed empty cups into a garbage bag.

"Oh," I said, surprised.

He stopped and looked at me. "Why? Did it not do that?"

"What? No! It did that. It did more than that," I said, letting the words slip from my lips.

I watched a smile appear on his lips. We finished up, and I walked him to the front door. As I opened it, my face contorted with shock and confusion.

Standing on my front steps was Danny and Liz making out.

"Oh, my God," I gasped.

They stopped and gave me a cheeky grin. "Oh, hey Patty," they both greeted me.

I took a step down, "Don't hey Patty me! What is going on here?"

"Well, since you hooked up with one of my friends, I thought I would return the favor," he smirked.

"Hooked up? We didn't hook up! We haven't even gone on our first date!" I said.

"Potato, potatoes, you still kissed," he shrugged.

I stood there, and Nate chuckled. I guess this was a night of many surprises.

That was the most exciting birthday ever.

CHAPTER 16

FIRST DATE

Liz spent most of the week trying to get me to talk about what happened with her and Danny, but I brushed her off. It was weird. I never expected that and with my brother. I didn't want to think about it.

I prefer it if we never talked about them, ever. Plus, I had other things on my mind, like where Nate was taking me Friday night. I know he said dinner and a movie, but I was hoping it was nothing fancy. The extent of my fanciness comprised weddings when they forced me to wear a dress. Funerals, I could get away with wearing dress slacks.

It made me anxious, and I hadn't spoken to Nate since my birthday. More thoughts floated through my head with wondering if that night was a one-time thing. Ugh, I need to stop overthinking everything.

Luckily, when I requested Friday night off, they gave it to me. I usually work every weekend. God, I hope this date goes well, or it sucks, getting stood up.

Feeling anxious about going on a first date is bad enough. When it's with the neighbor guy you had a massive crush on growing up, it's ten times worse. On top of it, he's seven years older than me, which means he has much experience. Trust me; I've seen the girls he's dated. That made me feel even more nervous as Friday approached. Will someone shoot me?

After school on Friday, I hurried home. I still did not understand what to wear. Nate never told me the dress code.

I debated calling him but didn't want to appear to be the "needy" type. I didn't know what type I was. I mean, it's not like I had any experience in this thing. He said he wanted to take things slow. What does that exactly mean?

How slow does one take it? Is there a time length? Do we even know the definition of lazy? I'm sure I'm not the only girl that has questioned these things. Or I am, I didn't know.

Then there was the whole point of when do you get ready? How long should you take to get prepared? When do you even start?

It followed with more questions. Do I wait in my bedroom? Do I wait in the living room? Do I meet him at the front door? Am I too eager? Am I not keen enough? What if the date is an epic failure? Will this ruin our friendship? Will he hold my hand? Will he kiss me?

I was making myself neurotic with all these questions. Not only was I making myself an obsessive, but I also became a nervous wreck. Dating's not complicated.

I walked into my room and set my backpack on the floor, and they're lying on my bed was a dozen red roses and a note. I picked up the roses and inhaled the scent. I love roses; they were my favorite flower.

I laid them down and picked up the note. It read:

Patty

I wanted to do this right. So, I brought these for you, for when you got home. Here is something special for a special woman. Dress casual. The jeans are okay. I want you to feel comfortable. I'll be there around five to pick you up.

Nate

I smiled when I read his note. Wow, is all I can say. I glanced at the time. It was almost three, which gave me two hours to get ready. In reality, it only takes me forty-five minutes at the most. They always taught me to be on time.

Rule of thumb in our house if you weren't on time, you got left behind. It was an excellent rule to have.

I hopped in the shower and washed up. I shaved my underarms and legs. I don't know why since I would wear pants, but I felt like I needed to.

Then I dried off and dressed. I finished by fixing my hair and putting on some light makeup. Not too much, but enough to bring out my features. It took me years to learn how to wear makeup. The first time I ever tried it, I looked like a clown. Trust me; it wasn't pretty.

I finished with some time to spare, so I sat on my bed and watched TV pass the time. As the time drew near, so did my nerves. It was almost five o'clock, and my leg shook in anticipation, waiting on Nate. My big fear was he wouldn't show, ugh.

Then I heard a knock at my door. I stood up, and it opened up to my mom standing there.

"Hun, there is a very nice-looking guy waiting for you in the living room," she smiled.

I took a deep breath and grabbed my coat and purse. I walked past Mom, through the kitchen, and into the living room. Nate was sitting on the couch talking to Dad, uh, oh.

I walked in and looked at Nate. He's dressed in jeans, a black leather jacket, and wearing a chain bracelet on his left wrist. Holy hell, he was hot.

I cleared my throat, and he turned to see me. He stood up and straightened his jeans out.

"Ready?" He asked me with a smile.

"Yep," I answered with a more significant smile.

"See ya later, Mr. George," he waved to Dad.

"Take excellent care of her, Nate," he said.

I followed him out of the house, and we walked over to his car. I felt excited, more so now than nervous.

We got into the car, and Lucille ran over to the car. She knocked on his window, and he rolled it down.

"Yeah?" he asked her with a slight annoyance.

"Don't forget your raincoat. I don't need any grand-babies," Lucille reminded Nate as she handed him a condom. He rolled his eyes and snatched it from her hand. I turned beet red, and at that moment, I wanted to die. Only Lucille would do that.

He shoved it into the inner pocket of his coat and rolled up the window. Lucille waved, and he pulled out of the driveway. He drove to dinner.

"Sorry about ma," he sighed.

"It's Lucille. I expect it from her," I shrugged.

"At least you do. All the girls she met before would freak out at her."

"Made dating hard, huh?" I questioned him.

"It was a blessing in disguise," he smiled.

"Why?" I inquired.

"Because if they had worked out, I wouldn't be here with you," he answered, turning to look at me. I couldn't help but blush. Nate looked freaking hot. I used to see him with messy hair or dirty from working on cars; he looked terrific when he cleaned up.

He pulled into a Denny's, and we got out of the car, making our way inside. The hostess sat us in a booth and handed us menus. I looked through mine and figured out what I wanted to eat.

The waitress came over and took our orders. We talked while we waited for our meal.

"So, is this a good first date?" He asked me.

"Yeah, I would say so," I smiled.

"Good, because I wanted to make sure you had an excellent time."

"So far, so good. I wanted to thank you for the flowers. I loved them. Roses are my favorite flower," I said.

"I'm glad. I was trying to decide what to get you. I wasn't sure if I should get you roses or something else. It seems like roses are the main flower for most guys to give to women," he said to me.

"No, it was perfect. It helped. I was a little nervous," I confessed.

He chuckled. "You're parents said you were mumbling a lot when you got home. I figured it was because of nerves."

The waitress brought our food. We ate and talked more.

"It's hard going from being neighbors to something more, you know? You're seven years older and thought about you having all this experience. I had none. You call it a day afterward." I was rambling and was thinking of ways to stop myself.

"Patty," Nate spoke in a calm voice, getting my attention.

"Yeah?" I looked at him.

"I don't care that you don't have any experience or that you're seven years younger. I like you a lot. Sitting on your picnic table behind your house at night and talking made me like you even more. It gave me a chance to get to know you for you," he said. I relaxed once he said that. It was reassuring to know that my inexperience or age difference didn't matter to him.

With that, I could relax and enjoy the date. We finished dinner, and once Nate paid the bill, we left for the movies.

Nate let me pick the movie, and I chose The American President. We found our seats and sat down. I rested my hands on the armrests, and we talked until the movie started. It was lovely sitting there with him.

The lights dimmed until it became dark, and the movie started. As I sat there, I felt Nate's hand touch mine. He slid his hand into mine and intertwined our fingers. I leaned my head against his shoulder and resting on it. He maneuvered himself, pulling his hand away from mine and wrapping his arm around me.

His cologne on him smelled pleasant, and I inhaled the scent, getting lost in it. I cuddled into him, and we watched a movie like that.

After the movie, we got up as he took my hand, holding it as we left the theater. We walked to the car hand in hand. He opened my door, and I climbed in, then he shut it. He walked around to the driver's side and climbed inside.

He took me home and pulled into my driveway. We got out of the car, and he walked me to my front door, hand in hand.

I turned to him. "Thank you for tonight."

He looked at me and smiled. "Any time." Then he reached up and placed a finger under my chin and pulled my lips to his, giving me a sweet kiss. I wrapped my arms around his neck as I kissed him back.

I pulled back and suggested, "We should do this again."

"Definitely," he said, giving me another kiss then walking back to his car.

I ran into the house to find Mom waiting up for me.

"Well," he asked me.

"Best date ever. Night," I answered, grinning as I went to my room. She laughed.

Tonight was the best, and Nate wasn't what I expected. He was so much more.

CHAPTER 17

I HAD A GOOD TIME

I woke up the next morning with a smile on my face. Last night was terrific, and so was Nate. The date was memorable. Ugh, I hated it to the end.

I heard the phone ringing, and my mom answered it. Then she knocked on my door.

"Come in," I yelled to her.

She opened the door and said, "Phone for you." She handed me the phone, and I took it. She left, closing the door behind her.

"Hello?" I answered.

"Hey, I wanted to tell you I had a glorious time last night," Nate said to me.

"I did too," I agreed.

"What are you doing right now?" He asked me.

"Lying in bed, in my PJs," I replied.

"Oh?" He responded.

"Get your mind out of the gutter," I replied as I rolled my eyes. I heard Nate chuckle on the other end.

"So, does that mean you're lazy today?"

"Depends."

"On what?"

"On if someone can persuade me not to be lazy or they can come over, and we can be lazy together," I suggested.

"Or someone can come over here so we can cuddle under a blanket and have a movie marathon."

"Hmmm, I like your idea better."

"I thought you would. Plus, my parents are going to my aunt's today."

"Where are your brothers at?"

"They're both working."

"Wow, Cayson finally got a job?"

"Shocking, isn't it?" He chuckled.

I laughed in response to him.

"Well, I have to get dressed and eat breakfast," I said.

"I thought you could come over in your PJs," he spoke.

"Dad would never allow it," I reminded him.

"Oh, right, never mind? How about this? You get a dress. I'll take you to breakfast, and then we'll have a movie marathon?"

"You had me at breakfast." He chuckled on the other end. We hung up, and I changed my clothes. I pulled on my coat and replaced the phone on the base. I let Mom know what I was doing before I left. Her answer to me was, "Have fun."

I opened my front door and stepped outside. The air had gotten colder, and a sharp, stiff breeze blew over me. I shivered at the coldness. I hated fall weather this late, and I don't consider November fall. It feels like winter. There are four months for winter, November, December, January, and February in Michigan. It's freaking cold.

Nate backed out of his driveway and pulled into mine. I got in, closing the door, and shivered.

"Cold?"

"Y-yes," I said as my teeth chattered away. Nate chuckled as I tried to warm myself while trying to buckle my seatbelt. Have you ever tried buckling a belt when your hands are ice cold? It's hard.

He drove us to Coney Island to have breakfast. We got out of the car, and I didn't wait for him. I ran into the restaurant. He caught up to me. "Thanks for leaving me."

"Psh, you'll get over it," I replied as I tried to warm myself. The waitress seated us, and I kept my coat on until I warmed up. We ordered breakfast and talked.

"What did your mom say when you told her?" He asked me.

"Have fun. Mom's not worried about me going out with an older guy," I joked with him.

"Because she knows I would do nothing to disrespect you. No offense, but my ma may be crazy, but yours is hella scary when she's mad."

"Really?" I questioned him.

"Yeah, I've seen her lose her shit with you two," he commented to me, causing me to laugh. My mom has lost her shit with Danny and me. Dad got to come home to hear all about it. It was never pretty.

The waitress brought us our food, and I dug in. I was starving. Plus, I love breakfast.

"So, what movies are we watching?"

"Some action, comedy, or anything that piqued our interest," he answered between bites.

"Sounds good to me. Do your parents know?"

"Nope, I didn't need ma to shove another condom at me," he said as I giggled.

"That was funny."

"Says the girl who turned three shades of red. We had our first date. I'm not that fast," he said.

"I had a splendid time last night," I mentioned.

"So, do I. It's been a while since I took a girl on the first date," he smiled.

Him saying that made me smile. We finished our breakfast and then went back to his house. When we got there, we ran inside. He took off his coat and tossed it over a chair as I did the same.

He put some logs in their fireplace and started a fire. I sat down on the couch. He popped in a movie and walked over to the couch, taking a seat behind me. He pulled me against him, so I was sitting between his legs, laying with my back against his chest. He pulled a blanket off of the end of the couch, covering us with it.

He wrapped his arms around me, tangling his legs around mine. I could feel his chest move in a smooth movement. It was relaxing. I snuggled into him, and we watched the movie.

As I lay there, he took his hands and rubbed the top of my hands with his fingers. It was beautiful, the two of us sitting there. Nate didn't make me feel uncomfortable. He was gentle with me, and I appreciated it.

At some point, I fell asleep. I don't know how long I slept, but I was lying on Nate's chest, who was also sleeping when I woke up. I looked up at him. I noticed his sharp jawline and how his hair flopped on his forehead as he slept. He looked peaceful.

I reached up and dabbed his face with my finger, tracing it, making my way to his lips. The minute my finger touched his lips, he kissed it. He opened an eye. "Hey," he said.

"Hi," I said to him.

"Did you have a good nap?"

"It was the best nap ever," I stretched.

"Yeah, I thought so too. See, I have this sweet girl that I can snuggle up to like a teddy bear."

"Oh, you do, do you?" I said.

"Yeah, it's nice."

I smiled as he reached up, pulling my lips closer to his until he was kissing me. He released my lips and smiled. "I like it slow."

"Good, because I don't think I can go fast, even if I wanted to," I said.

"Fine by me," he shrugged.

I sat until I was sitting on his legs. I rubbed my eyes and yawned. I looked around. It seemed weird with no one here except us. I usually saw Lucille being here.

I got up, and he looked at me, confused.

"Where are you going?"

I smiled and said, "Bathroom. I have to pee." He laughed as I walked to the bathroom. I got done and came out to see him still on the couch. I walked back over and took a seat next to him.

"Another movie?" He suggested to me.

"Yep, except there is one thing."

"What's that?" He asked me.

"I'm hungry," I said as he chuckled.

"Okay, hang on, I'll make us some sandwiches," he said, getting up. I got up and followed him to the kitchen.

He pulled out lunch meat, lettuce, tomatoes, cheese, and mayo. I got some plates down, and he made two sandwiches, one for him and one for me. Then he grabbed a bag of chips and carried them over to the table. I grabbed some glasses and poured us something to drink.

We sat down and ate.

"That's one thing I like about you," he said, taking a bite of his sandwich.

"What's that?"

"You eat. Most girls won't eat because they are afraid the guy makes fun of them."

"I'm sorry, but if a guy can't stand to watch me eat, he best moves along because I love food," I said to him, popping a chip in my mouth.

"Trust me; I prefer a girl to eat. It's unnatural when they don't," he said.

"Sleep and food, my two ultimate goals in life," I smirked, making him laugh.

"You like both, don't you?"

"I do. Both are wonderful things," I sighed.

Sitting there, having lunch with Nate, and having a conversation felt so natural and right. He was funny and easy to talk to when he spoke more than a few words at a time. Grunts not included.

We finished our lunch and went back to our movie marathon. Nate spending time with me was fun with kisses thrown in here and there, but he kept it simple. I was thankful for that.

I didn't think this would become more once Lucille got involved. I had a feeling she was up to no good again.

CHAPTER 18

LUCILLE IS AT IT AGAIN

When Lucille wants something, she wants something. How did she persuade my parents to let me go with Nate up to their family cabin is beyond me? Even better is how she got me to agree to go. I still can't comprehend how that happened? I don't think I want to.

The woman called my boss, telling him that there was a death in the family; I was going out of town for the weekend. I got many sympathies. I prefer not to lose some crazy uncle I never met and who didn't exist.

Nate pulled up to a cabin, and we grabbed our bags out of the back seat. I walked up and looked at it. It was a wooden cabin out in the middle of nowhere. That wasn't creepy at all.

"So, why are we here again?" I asked him.

"Ma thought we could get the cabin ready for when they come up hunting Thanksgiving weekend."

"Do you hunt?"

"Nope, no interest in it," he said, walking up the steps onto the porch. The boards creaked under our feet as he opened the door and felt around for a light switch. He flipped the switch, and a light turned on.

It was your typical cabin. There was a living room, kitchen area, bedrooms, and bathrooms. Thank God for that. I hated outhouses. I had to use a few, and they were gross. Plus, you had to watch for spiders and any other insect that made it their home.

He showed me around and then showed me to a bedroom. It was okay. I mean, it had a bed and a dresser. Nothing fancy.

After getting settled in, I changed into some comfy clothes and slippers. Nate looked at my footwear and chuckled. "Nice slippers," he commented.

I looked down at my pink fuzzy slippers. "Don't judge. They're comfy."

"I bet," he snickered. I rolled my eyes and went to the fridge. I wanted something to eat, then get some sleep since we would clean all weekend.

We finished our meals, and I made my way to bed. I know most people would jump at the chance to be alone with each other, but Nate and I got together. We haven't even made it official, and I wasn't anywhere near that point.

Luckily, he understood. Or I would be in deep shit. I crawled into bed and pulled the blankets over me, then I rolled over and turned out the lights. I shivered, trying to find warmth. It was freezing up here.

As I tried to get warm, I felt the bed dip on the other side of me. Then the covers moved, and before I knew it, I felt two arms wrap around me. So much for sleeping in separate beds.

"Um, Nate?"

"Mmm?"

"Why are you in here?"

"Because it's freezing."

"Okay." I let out a slight whimper.

He leaned into my ear. "It's okay. I'm going to cuddle with you."

"That's all?"

"That's all," he answered.

I let out a sigh, and before I knew it, I fell asleep next to Nate in bed.

I opened my eyes and rubbed them. I turned to see Nate sleeping next to me. His hair flopped over his forehead, and his mouth was open. I couldn't help but giggle a little. Most people think someone looks cute sleepy, but not with Nate. He looked funny.

I lay there until I heard a groan and movement next to me. I turned and saw Nate open his eyes halfway.

"Morning," he mumbled.

"Morning," I smirked.

"Why are you up?"

"Unknown place, an unused bed," I shrugged.

"Well, get used to it with us dating," he mumbled.

"I guess," I said, looking around.

His head popped up. "You guess?"

"What?"

He got up, and before I had time to react, he engulfed my body with his, hovering over me. "Oh, there's no guessing about us."

"Us? I was talking about an unknown place, you dink," I said, poking his forehead with my index finger.

"Oh," he replied.

I shook my head and rolled my eyes. "Are you always this possessive of the girls you date?"

"Only the ones I'm serious with," he said to me.

"We started dating. We aren't even an official couple yet, and you're already laying claim to me?"

"When you put it that way, yes, I am," he shrugged. I let out a giggle. "When the time is right, we'll make it official."

I couldn't help but smile. "Okay, can you get off of me?" I pushed him off of me, causing him to land on his back on the bed.

As I got up, he grabbed my wrist and pulled me back on top of him. "Oh, I don't think so. You owe me a kiss." He pulled me into a kiss and deepened it. I kissed him back.

I pulled back and looked at him. "Much better," he said to me. I couldn't help but smile.

This time we both got up and had breakfast with Nate cooking, which kind of surprised me. I offered to cook, but he said he would.

Once he finishes, he puts the food on the plates, and we sat down at the island and ate. It was great.

"What?" He asked me.

"I didn't know you knew how to cook. I figure cars were your specialty." I said.

"I know how to cook, clean, work on cars. You name it, I've learned it."

"Do your brothers know how to cook?"

"Yeah, ma figure we should learn, so we don't starve," he smirked. I let out a giggle.

"I have a feeling she didn't send us here to clean since the place looks good," he said, looking around.

Then it hit me, Lucille. I should have known she was behind all this. I slapped my head.

"What?"

"Your mom did this on purpose."

"What do you mean?"

"It's all making sense now."

"What is?"

"Everything is. Your mom has wanted us to get together forever. Do you know that when I was fifteen, she said she was hoping we would get together? She was hoping it would put you on the strait and narrow?"

He looked at me and started laughing. "Good ole ma, always plotting and planning," he said, chuckling.

I shook my head at that.

"But for what it's worth, I'm glad," he said, reaching over to me and tucking a loose strand of hair behind my head.

"I am too. You surprised me," I said to Nate.

"Why's that?"

"Because you made all my firsts were amazing so far. Most girls get disasters for their firsts, but mine was outstanding," I said with a smile.

"I'm glad. I was a little nervous when I took you out."

"Why?"

"Because you weren't like the girls I dated before. Knowing you my entire life, you have always been special to me. At four years old, you told everyone I was your boyfriend," he reminded me.

"That's right," I said, thinking about it. "But you never denied it. You said, 'Yes, I was Patty's boyfriend.' You were eleven," I added with a slight laugh.

"I didn't want to hurt your feelings, so I played along with it. Then I watched you grow up from this tomboyish kid to the beautiful woman you are today. You blossomed," he said.

"Well, if we're honest. When you showed up for our date, you looked incredible. I was so used to you looking dirty and your hair a mess that to see you all cleaned up and looking nice was unbelievable."

He chuckled at that.

"I didn't think you wanted to go on a date with me if I looked like a scrub."

"True, but either way, I loved everything about that night. It was perfect," I said to him. I was swooning over him at that moment.

"Good, because this makes dating you so much easier," he said to me. That made me smile even more significant if that was possible.

Being here with him felt like we were in this tiny bubble, the two of us. There are no outside influences because it's him and me. I loved it. I knew it wouldn't last, and we would have to be in the actual world.

The surprising thing was my parents didn't object to Nate, and I am dating. I figure they would have an issue with it more than anyone, but they didn't because they knew the Grays. They knew them since they moved into the house kitty-corner from them. Also, that they were well mannered didn't hurt.

I guess that's what bothered me when people commented about them because I saw them. They were respectful, funny, smart, and incredible. They developed a reputation as troublemakers over the years.

While most people saw them like that, I saw them as more. I saw them as friends who would do anything for you. Their loyalty was like no other. For that, I admired them.

The rest of the time we were at the cabin, we cleaned even though it wasn't dirty and spent time together. It was great.

We ended up sleeping in the same bed, but Nate did nothing I wasn't ready for or comfortable with yet. As he said, he enjoys taking it slow. I didn't mind and preferred it. It took much pressure off me.

Trust me, I've heard horror stories of girls doing things they weren't ready for yet. That was one reason I shy away from dating. I didn't want or need the extra pressure that most guys put on girls, especially sex. Sex can wait.

CHAPTER 19

DATING A GRAY BOY

Dating a Gray boy came with more than I realized. It was cool.

Nate would take me out, or I would have dinner at his house, or he would have dinner at mine. When I wasn't working, he would spend time with me, even if that meant distracting me from homework. I would slug him. I wasn't about to let my grades fall.

At work, he would find an excuse to come into the store so he could see me. Lucille was good at that. Being with Nate was terrific, but nothing beats the night we were out and ran into Brian and Tricia.

We stood in the movie's lobby theater, looking at the list of movies playing. We were trying to decide what to see when I heard someone say, "Oh look, the trash is taking out the trash."

We turned around, and Brian and Tricia stood there. She snickered as we looked at them. I frowned, and I could feel Nate tense. Shit. He has a temper, and any minute it was about to blow.

Brian walked over to me. "I told you, hanging out with them does nothing but bring you down."

Then something unexpected happened. Nate slid his hand into mine and intertwined our fingers. He gave it a gentle squeeze, and as soon as I squeezed it back, he relaxed. It was at that moment that I understood what Lucille meant. Damn, she's smart.

I looked at him, then at Brian, "No, Brian, the only trash here is you. See, while you walk around thinking you're all that, Nate is, and he doesn't have to prove it. One day, we won't be in high school. All those who follow you leave because you're no longer going to be the high man on the totem pole. But with Nate, he knows that. So, say whatever you want, but I have someone that already knows what he wants in life. Enjoy sponging off of your rich girlfriend, ta, ta."

I turned, and while still holding Nate's hand, I led him away from Brian. He stopped, and I turned to him, giving him a confused look until he pulled me to him. He pressed his lips against mine, kissing me, then let go of my hand and placed them on my face. I reached up and put my hands on his back.

Brian and Tricia stood there in shock.

He pulled back and looked at them. "So that you know, Patty's one hell of a kisser." He shot them a wink and then dropped his arms, taking my hand and walking to the ticket booth.

Yeah, I hadn't told many people I was dating a Gray boy. Guess the cat is out of the bag now.

After seeing the looks on their faces that night, I couldn't help but smile. It was priceless.

I sat in my room, reliving Friday events all over again, and my smile got bigger and bigger. Then my door busted open with Liz exclaiming, "Why didn't you tell me you were dating Nate Gray?"

"Hello to you too," I said, arching an eyebrow.

"Yeah, yeah, hi," she said, waving me off. She walked over and sat down on my bed. "Is that why I haven't seen you in forever, except at school?" Her look on her face said it all.

I sighed. "Yes, but I was also working too."

"So, tell me everything," she demanded.

"What's there to say? He's amazing."

She looked to see the vase of red roses on my dresser. "Amazing? The guy gave you roses."

I looked at the flowers she was pointing to on my dresser.

"Those? Those would be new. The other ones had died," I said.

"Other ones? Damn!"

"He knows they're my favorite flower, so he replaces them when they die," I shrugged. I don't know why I was acting so relaxed about it. I guess I enjoyed keeping it private. It was like a guilty pleasure for me.

"So, have you guys, you know?"

I looked at her with a weird look. "No," I answered.

"Why not?"

"Because we're taking it slow, and he's not like that."

"Patty, the dude is twenty-four. He's an experience. How long do you think he'll wait?"

"I don't know, but we already talked about it, and he's fine with going slow. Liz, being with Nate, isn't about sex. We talk, we laugh, we enjoy each other. Plus, he treats me with respect," I said.

"Okay, so why haven't you told anyone that you two are dating?" It was a simple question.

"Because it's none of their business, the people that know are my family and his. How did you find out?"

"Danny, let it slip."

I gave her a look. I still didn't like the fact that my brother and my best friend were seeing each other. There wasn't anything I could do about it.

"He did," I sighed, rubbing my forehead in frustration.

She reached over and touched my arm. "Patty, if Nate treats you well, then that's all that matters." She reassured me.

"He does. He does. But I'm also a little scared."

"Why?"

"Because I'm falling in love with him," I said, looking at her. She looked at me, stunned. That was the difference between most girls and me. When I liked someone or cared about them, I developed serious feelings for them, which scared the hell out of me.

My door opened, and we both looked up to see Nate standing there. Oh god, how long has he been standing there? We looked at his face, and I couldn't tell if it was horror or anger. Great, I blew it.

"I hear Danny calling me," she got up from my bed. She looked at me then at him and said, "Bye." She bolted out of my room.

I stood up and started rambling. "Look, I'm sorry. It's that Liz was asking me questions and I didn't know what to say. Then the conversation changed, and before I knew it, the words slipped out. But I understand if this is too much," I said as he strolled towards me.

As he walked towards me, I backed until my back hit the wall, and he was inches from my face. I stared at him, and he looked at me, "So, you think you're falling in love with me?"

"Um, yes," was all I could get out.

"And you like that I respect you and are taking it slow?"

"Y-yes," I stuttered.

"Huh, then I guess there's only one thing to say." He leaned in and whispered, "I love you."

He leaned back, and my eyes widened as I stared at him.

"What?"

"You heard me."

"Y-you l-love me?" I didn't know why I was stuttering like a damn fool.

"Well, I wanted to do this, you know, ask you to be my girl then tell you, but things have been backward with us." He smirked, and I looked at him.

His girl? Would he ask me to be his girl? Would this make us an official couple? Those words kept ringing through my head, his girl.

All I could think was the inner me was doing one hell of a merry dance.

"Are you asking me to be your girlfriend?"

"Well, that's what asking you to be my girl usually means," he countered me.

I didn't know what to say. Here Nate told me he loved me and asked me to be his girlfriend, and I was speechless.

"Well," he asked. I could tell he was getting impatient, waiting for me to respond.

"What would you do if I said yes?" I looked at his expression as he studied my face trying to gauge what his reaction would be.

He reached over and placed his hand on my cheek, running his thumb over my bottom lip, playing with it. "I guess I would do this." He leaned in and kissed me. My lips parted when he did that. He slipped his tongue past my lips into my mouth, swirling around with mine.

He had one hand placed on the wall next to my head. He put the other on my waist, pulling me so close, it closed any gaps between us. As our tongues swirled and our bodies molded to each other, it was by far the most intense kiss we had. The boy knows what he is doing.

I couldn't get enough of the way he kissed me. It was like my lips yearned to have his on them. He pulled back, leaving them swollen from the pressure he applied. I reached up and touched them, feeling the feeling that was left behind.

He moved a loose strand behind my ear, and I looked at him. "Yes," I said as I watched his lips curl upward into a smile. Even though it hadn't been a month since we started dating, I couldn't help but feel like this was the right decision for me.

Nate wasn't a childhood crush I had for years; he became so much more to me. Everything he did with me or for me was exceptional in every sense. Nate took great care of me and the things I liked. He was also easy on the eyes. What? Don't judge. Nate was hot.

He looked at me. "You do not understand how happy I am right now."

"I do."

"You do?" He looked at me, confused.

"Yes, because I'm thrilled myself," I smiled. Nate pulled me into another mind-blowing kiss. I could get used to this.

CHAPTER 20

'TIS THE SEASON

Nate and I made things official, and our families knew. Lucille and Mom started conspiring together. What is with everyone conspiring with each other? I swear these people have nothing better to do with their time.

It was also a Christmas vacation, which meant doing all things Christmas. I helped them decorate their tree, and Nate helped decorate ours.

Lucille and Mom baked cookies together and roped me into helping them. They made all kinds of cookies. I like cookies, but around this time, I'm sick of them. As they baked and I decorated, the door to the garage opened up, and in walked Nate, dirty from work. He popped his head into the kitchen.

"Well, hello, Betty Crocker," he grinned.

"Hey, Grease monkey," I retorted. He laughed.

"I cleaned up, then I'll come help," he said as he went into the bathroom off to the side. I heard the shower turn on and went back to frosting cookies.

"Hey, Lucille?"

"Yeah?"

"I was thinking of getting something for Nate for Christmas. Do you think he would like a model car for Christmas?"

They both looked at me, and I looked at them. "What? Is it a terrible gift?"

"No, but why a model car?" Lucille asked me.

"Well, because I know he loves putting them together and the fact I broke a couple when I was younger. I figured it would be something he likes. Or not," I blurted. Damn. I should have thought this through. It was a horrible gift.

Before she could say anything, we heard the shower turn off. A few minutes later, Nate emerged in sweats, a tee-shirt, and socks. His wet hair hung down on his forehead. Looking at him, I knew my gift was a bust. The worst part I had already bought it.

I said no more about it. What's the point? Here I have a boyfriend who does thoughtful things for me, and I buy him a model car — some gift.

While most of the vacation, I worked and tried to get into the Christmas spirit. My mind kept wandering back to Nate's gift as I sat on my bed, staring at it. It's wrapped and had a red bow on it.

It tempted me to throw it away and figure something else out. I mean, what a stupid gift. I sighed.

I heard a knock at the door, and Nate says, "Patty?"

My eyes widened, and I got up, snatching the gift off of my dresser. As I held it in my hands, Nate opened my door. I looked down and immediately put it behind my back.

"What's that?" He questioned me.

"What's what?" I replied with another question, trying to act like I didn't know what he refers to what I'm holding in my hand.

"What do you have behind your back?" He asked me, pointing behind me.

"This? Oh, it's nothing," I smiled.

"What is it?" He walked over, closing the gap between us.

"It's nothing."

He reached behind me and pulled the gift from me. I tried to take it back, but he held it out of my reach. He looked at it. "To Nate from Patty, huh?"

"It's stupid," I mumbled.

"Can I open it?" He asked, turning to look at me.

"It's not Christmas. I plan on getting you something different," I huffed.

"Okay, then I can open it."

"Nate! Don't!" He tore open the gift and looked at it. I placed my hand on my face as I held my other arm around my waist.

"You bought me a model car?" He looked at me.

"It's dumb, I know. I saw it and thought you would like it because you always loved putting together model cars, growing up. Then when I asked your mom, she looked at me like I was an idiot. I'm sorry it's such a simple gift. I'm a horrible girlfriend," I mumble, shifting my eyes from his face to my feet. He looked at the gift and then looked at me. "It's outstanding."

My head snapped up. "What?"

"The gift you gave me. It's outstanding. You bought me something I love."

"So, you're not mad about it being a cheesy model car?"

"Mad? Why would I be mad? No girl has ever thought about me like this. All the other girls thought it was a stupid hobby," he sighed.

"But you always loved putting models together. You would sit for hours," I reminded him.

"Exactly, and you get that," he said to me. He reached over and took my hand. "Patty, you bought me something with me in mind. Something you knew I would love and enjoyed. That doesn't make a gift stupid; It makes it special. Because you thought of me."

I looked at him. I didn't know what to say. They always say it's the thought counts; I didn't realize what it meant until now. I wrapped my arms around his torso and buried my head into it. He wrapped his arms around me as I mumbled, "I love you."

"What?"

I lifted my head and looked into his eyes. "I said, I love you."

"Well, two gifts for the price of one. How about that?"

That was the first time I had told him I loved him. Even when he told me the first time, I never said it back. It had scared me. Hearing what he said about my gift made me realize that I loved him.

Three simple words, but with so much meaning behind them. How could I not love Nate? Nate has shown me so much in ways of caring about someone. He never pushed me into doing something I wasn't comfortable with him. He enjoys listening to me — age matters. I would take him being older any day of the week than a guy my age.

"Now, I came over to see if you wanted to go for a drive. The city is having a light festival," he said to me.

"Hmm, being in a warm car with you and looking at pretty lights? Sounds good to me." I smiled.

"That's what I thought. Go grab your coat," Nate said, and I let go of him so I could put on my coat.

He grabbed ahold of my coat and zipped it up for me, letting his fingers linger a little longer. I felt light-headed and excited all at the same time. I'm sure I was fangirling over him.

"Come on, Betty Crocker, we have some lights to look at," he said, taking my hand and leading me out of my room. Looking at Nate was blissful, not to mention he smelled amazing. Yep, I got it bad for the oldest Gray boy.

He drove to the light festival, and we got out of the car. Wait. I thought we were staying in the car? Damn it.

"Nate!"

"What?" He yelled.

"I thought we were staying in the car where there is heat! It's twenty degrees outside!" I exclaimed.

"It's forty!" He said.

"Feels like twenty," I grumbled to him.

"I guess that means you must cuddle close, now, won't it?" He smirked.

"Fine, but you're buying me hot cocoa for this," I said, pointing my finger at him.

"A hot chocolate beverage and cuddling with a desirable girl, fine by me," he shrugged. For it has only been forty degrees outside. My body heated. Well, shit.

Luckily, he had an extra pair of gloves and a hat. Although the hat was way too big, and I looked ridiculous in it. At least it's warm.

We walked over and purchased two hot cocoas to drink while looking at the lights. I took mine and took small sips. I used the cup to warm my hands.

Then we heard someone say, "I thought we would find you here." We turned to see his family there.

"Well, Betty Crocker here was having issues with the cold," he smirked.

"Yeah, well, he made me think we were staying in the car," I said with an annoyed look. They snickered.

It wasn't until I realized Grayson was with them. Oh, dear God, I had met him a few times, but he was always working.

Grayson Gray is a no-nonsense man. He was always taking his boys in hand because they were still getting into trouble. He was tall and built with steel-grey eyes like Nate. Nate was a mini version of his dad.

He had a gruffness about him that scared the living daylights out of people. Knowing the man he is, I'm sure he disapproved of the age difference between Nate and me.

Then he did something unexpected.

"Patty?"

"Huh, what?"

"I asked if you were having an enjoyable time?" Grayson said to me.

"Oh, yep, the best," I blurted. I didn't know what to say to the man.

"Can I have a word with you?"

"Oh, uh," I didn't get to finish before the boys shoved towards their father. Thanks. Nothing enjoys feeding me to the lion.

We walked away from them, and he turned to me. "So, I hear you and my son have been dating and are a couple."

"Well, it looks that way."

He stared at me. "I say this once, so listen up." My eyes widened. "I like it. You're an honorable person, and Lucille speaks well of you, as does the rest of the boys."

"Okay." Where was he going with this?

"You're a beneficial influence on Nathaniel, and I approve of this."

"So, it doesn't bother you that there is an age gap?" I couldn't help but ask.

"No, girls are more mature than boys. Plus, I watched you grow up," he said to me.

Whew, I thought to myself.

"Patricia, take excellent care of my boy," he said to me as he walked away. What the hell?

Nate walked over to me shortly after. "What was that about?"

"Your dad gave me his blessing to be with you," I said to him, stunned.

"That's a first," Nate commented.

"What do you mean?"

"Dad has never approved of any girl I brought home. Ma tolerated them. But you, well, you're something special," he smiled.

My cheeks heated, and he turned me to face him. He wrapped his arms around my neck and looked at me. "And you're mine."

I looked at him and smiled. Hearing him say, you're mine, made me realize how serious this was. I didn't care because I loved being Nate's. It was enough.

CHAPTER 21

'TIS THE SEASON, PART 2

I have to say this has been the best Christmas vacation I ever had, well, except at work. Working at a grocery store around the holidays is nuts. You would figure people would be happy, but they seem more miserable than anything.

Stocking shelves only to have people plow into you sucks. I swear Santa is bringing them coal in their stockings.

"Um, excuse me, miss. We wondered if you could help us find the tinsel."

Tinsel? Who the hell goes to the grocery store looking for tinsel? I looked up and gave them a look.

"Tinsel? Really? You know this a grocery store, right?"

"Yeah, Cayson's not too bright," Jonas smirked, and Cayson smacked him.

"Ignore my idiot brothers. They know not what they speak of," Nate said, rolling his eyes.

"I guess," I remarked.

"What time do you get off?"

"Around eleven, things have been so busy with Christmas the past few days. But it's extra money for school," I said.

"Okay, then we'll be back by eleven to pick you up," he said to me.

"I brought my car."

"Okay, fine, but after work, I'm coming over," he said with a look.

"And risk waking my dad, no way. I'll see you after I check in with my mom," I said to him.

He gave me a quick kiss and left with his brothers. I finished my shift and went when one guy at work offered to walk me to my car. I declined, and they shrugged.

I buttoned up my coat and went out to my car. As I went to put the key into the lock, someone grabbed me. I didn't have time to react before they hit me, then hit me again. I tried to fight back, but it only made them angrier as they tore at my clothes, ripping them.

I reached into my pocket and pulled out my little spray bottle of pepper spray, spraying them in the eyes. As they screamed, I pushed them off me as I hurried, getting into my car. I drove out of there as fast as I could.

On my way home, I was having a hard time seeing through the tears. Instead of going back, I pulled into the Grays driveway. I got out and ran to their door, pounding on it.

"Please! Open up," I cried as I pounded on it.

Jonas opened the door. "Patty?" He looked at me, shocked. "What happened?"

"I went to my car. This guy grabbed me, hit me, and ripped my clothes." I was so hysterical I couldn't get the words out.

"Jonas! It's freezing. Close the door," Cayson yelled, walking to the door when he spotted me. "Patty?"

"Nate," I cried.

"Come here," Jonas said to me, then turned to Cayson, "go get Nate, now," ordering him.

He pulled me to him and helped me inside.

"Patty? Oh, dear God," Lucille exclaimed when she saw me.

Then I heard Nate yell, "What the hell?"

"Ma, can you take care of her? We have some business to take care of," Jonas told her, handing me off to his mother.

"Sure, come here, sweetie," she said, taking me into the bathroom as I cried. I heard the door close, knowing the boys were on their way to find who did this.

They pulled up to find the guy trying to clean his eyes with the snow.

"Must be the guy," Jonas commented to them.

"Must not be his lucky day," Nate growled.

They pulled up and got out. Nate picked him up and hit him over and over. "You think you can hurt a woman and get away with it? Especially my woman! You're a piece of shit!" He hit him, causing him to land on the ground on his back.

Cayson walked over. "Hey, I know this guy. He works here."

"Good, now we can have them call the police," Nate said, yanking him up and dragging him to the store. He dragged him to the counter and tossed the guy down, alerting everyone.

"What's going on here?" The manager asked.

"It seems one of your employees attacked another employee," Nate told them.

"What?" the manager responded, shocked.

"Yeah, he hit her and tore her clothing," Jonas told him.

"Which employee?"

"Patricia George, you know Joan George's daughter," Cayson answered.

"Christ," the manager grumbled.

"Either have the police handle it, or I will," Nate offered to him.

He turned to a lady. "Call the police."

With that, the three of them left.

I heard the door open, and I looked to see the three of them standing in the bathroom doorway. Lucille was cleaning up the blood and putting bandaids on me.

I stared at Nate as she did this, and he stared back at me. She looked at me. "Okay, I got everything," she replied, holding my chin with her palm and checking me over.

"I'll call your mom," she said, getting up.

As she walked with the boys, Jonas asked, "What are you going to tell them?"

"The truth that someone hurt their daughter. One time, a parent needs to know the truth about their child," she answered as she walked away.

Nate walked in, and I kept my eyes on him. I didn't smile or talk. I looked at him. He knelt in front of me with a worried look and then pulled me to him. He wrapped his arms around me, and I cried. I felt him stroke the back of my head as I cried.

I felt humiliated and upset. It was one thing to round with Brian, but it was another to have some guy grab you. I never felt so scared in my entire life.

I heard a knocking at the front door and then muffled voices. I looked up to see Mom and Dad standing there. They walked over to me, and Dad took Nate's place.

"Dad?" My voice broke.

"It's okay," he reassured me in his deep voice, causing me to cry. Sometimes a girl needs her father to tell her everything is okay. "Come on, let's get you home."

I nodded as we stood up, and he wrapped his arm around me while I held onto him.

Nate walked over to my mom. "Can I come?"

She sighed. "Yes," she told Nate. With that, he followed her out.

That night changed my life in a way I never thought was possible. It made me realize that no matter what, anything can and happen to you.

My parents threatened legal action against the store for them to relent. They let me have some time off until I felt ready to go back. All you have to say is the word lawyer, and people do whatever you want.

Christmas Eve arrived, and I didn't want to be festive. The fact I had a broken nose and two black eyes didn't help. I sat on the couch, watching Christmas movies to help take my mind off things, when there was a knock at the door.

"I'll get it," Danny yelled.

I heard muffled voices, and the front door to the living room opened, and in walked Nate. He sat down next to me on the couch.

"What are we watching?" He leaned over and whispered.

"A Christmas Story," I answered him.

"Ah, an excellent choice in a movie, classic and funny," he said, bobbing his head. A small smile formed upon my lips. "I wanted to show you something."

He turned away, and when he turned around, he was wearing a Santa Hat. I couldn't help but laugh. "So, could I pass for a jolly old elf?"

"More like a ridiculous elf," I giggled.

"Yeah, but it got you to laugh, didn't it?"

I reached over and grabbed his hand. "Yeah, it did. Thank you."

"I know you've been down ever since what happened, but Patty, it'll be okay," Nate reassured me.

At that moment, I couldn't help but cry. Nate pulled me to him as my family walked in and saw him comfort me. I grabbed his jacket and held it tight.

"I don't want to be afraid anymore, Nate. Please make it stop," I sobbed.

"It will. It's going to take time," Nate said, rubbing my back. He pulled me back and looked at me. "That's why you have me, my brothers, your brother, Liz, and everyone else to be there for you. Understand?"

I nodded and cuddled into him. I didn't want to fear to hold me captive. If it wasn't for the pepper spray, things could have gone so much worse for me. Thinking back, I should have taken him up on his offer to give me a ride home. If I did, I wouldn't be in the state I am today.

Nate stayed with me all night, and I fell asleep on him while we watched Christmas movies. The nightmares started. I woke up screaming, causing everyone to wake startled.

"Patty?" Nate looked at me with concern.

"Don't touch me! Stop! Please stop!" I was having full-fledged night terrors. Dad grabbed me and held me as I realized what happened.

"Patty, it's okay," Dad comforted me while looking at me.

"Hit." I couldn't form sentences with everything chaotic with my emotions.

He looked at Nate, "Rub her back." Nate started rubbing my back, and Dad got me to focus. "Patty, please look at me. It was only a nightmare. The guy won't hurt you. You are home safe, we're here, and so is Nate."

I nodded, knowing he was telling me the truth.

"Go sleep in the bed with your mom," he suggested to me. I got up and walked with Mom into their room and crawled into my parents' bed. Anytime I had nightmares growing up, I would crawl into my parents' bed with my mom. They would disappear so I could sleep.

Nate looked at my dad. "What was that?"

"They're night terrors. Patty would have horrible dreams. When she is under much emotional stress, she develops night terrors," Dad explained to him.

"How did it stop?"

"Well, Joan was the only one that could calm her, and then she started writing stories, many stories."

"She writes?"

"Developed it as a hobby when she was twelve and ended up loving it. But it helped."

"Good to know." He looked. "I'll head home. I'll see you guys tomorrow after we open gifts."

"Night, Nate," Dad said to him.

He got up and left. It would be an interminable night.

Christmas came, and we opened gifts. No one mentioned the night terror, which I was grateful for them not doing. As we opened presents, there was a knock at the door, and Danny let Nate in. I stood up and walked over to him. "Merry Christmas, Betty Crocker," he wished me.

"Merry Christmas, grease monkey." I kissed him, and he walked in. He took off his coat and handed me a gift.

"I wanted to get you something, and my ma suggested this."

I opened it, and it was a leather-bound journal. I looked at Nate.

"Your dad told me you love to write. I'm glad he did because I would have felt like this was a simple gift," he smiled.

I smiled. "I love it. Thank you." I kissed him, and we took a seat on the couch. I cuddled up next to him, and before I knew it, I fell asleep.

As the snow fell outside, they watched me sleep and in his arms. I held the leather-bound journal that Nate bought me. The one thing that would help my night terrors. I could not love him more for rescuing me from the demons that invaded my dreams. For that, I would be forever grateful.

CHAPTER 22

GUESS WHO'S BIRTHDAY IT IS?

After Christmas, I wrote in the journal as much as I could record my dreams and make brief stories out of them. Because of it, the nightmares became less when I could see what was haunting me in black and white. They call it a dream journal. Most doctors recommend it when you suffer a traumatic event.

I even let Nate read what I wrote, and it glued him to it.

"This is great," he commented to me.

"It's amazing what nightmares can do for you when you're writing," I said with a shrug.

He looked at me. "But it's getting better, right?"

"Yeah, it is," I said with a sigh.

"Patty? Talk to me."

I stood up, turned my back to him. Then turned to face him. "Even if the nightmares stop, I always feel like someone is following or watching me. It's unnerving," I said to him.

He set the journal on the bed and stood up. He placed his hands on my shoulders. "Patty, what you went through was traumatic, but the guy is in jail. They arrested him that night."

"Nate, he took my sense of security when he did that. The worst part is that I don't even know why?"

"What?" He looked at me.

"I do not understand why he did it. I didn't even know the guy," I said as a matter of fact.

"Are you sure?"

"Yes, why?"

"Because he works at the grocery store. Well, I used to work there."

"What?" I gave him a look.

"Cayson recognized him. They said his name was Shawn," he told me.

I sat down on the bed. My stomach churned.

"What is it?"

"When I was getting ready to leave, he offered to walk me to my car. I declined." I looked up at him with shock. He sat down next to me, and I looked at him. "Nate, I declined his offer because of you."

"It could have gone either way, whether you accepted or didn't. Luckily, you had pepper spray in your pocket," he reminded me.

"Because my mom is always harping on me to take it."

"Thank god for paranoid mothers," he smirked, causing me to giggle.

I didn't want to think about it anymore. It was making my stomach churn every time I did. So, I changed the subject.

"Isn't your birthday coming up?"

"Thanks for the reminder," he sighed.

"It's not that bad," I said, rolling my eyes.

"Since my ma has something planned, rethink that statement," he said.

"You're right," I said to him.

He gave me a look and pulled me into a kiss. He flipped me onto my back and crawled on top of me.

"I like this look on you."

"What look?"

"Me," he commented to me.

I laughed, and he kissed me again.

Lucille had a small party for Nate. Nothing extravagant, considering he didn't want to remind about turning twenty-five. I had purchased something little for him. I mean, what do you get a guy beside a model car to put together.

He opened his gifts; then, he opened mine. He pulled out an ID bracelet that I had his name engraved on it. He looked at it, then turned it over to see a date. I watched him as he smiled. "Really?"

"I felt it fit," I smirked.

"What did she have engraved underneath?" Jonas asked him.

He sat back and looked at me, shaking his head. "Her birthday," he mentioned.

"Why her birthday?" Cayson said.

"She knows why," Nate told them as he gave me a look.

"I don't get it," Jonas said.

I looked at Nate and said, "Because that was the day we shared our first kiss, which was on my birthday."

"Well, Nathaniel, now you never have a reason to forget when Patty's birthday is," Lucille said.

He glared at me, and I smirked at him. He shouldn't have given me my first kiss on my birthday. It's a win-win situation for me.

Later on, we were sitting on the couch eating cake, and he said, "Tell your mom, thanks for the cake."

"She didn't make it," I told him, taking a bite.

He turned and yelled, "Ma, did you make the cake?"

"Nope!"

He had a confused look on his face. "Who made the cake?"

"I did," I replied.

He gave me a look. "You can cook?"

"Yep, Mom taught me. Said to never rely on a man. Plus, I didn't want to starve if I ever get out on my own," I smiled.

"Good to know, you won't ever poison me when we get married," he mentioned.

I turned and looked at him. "Married," I said.

"I know you plan to go to school. You never told me where you're going."

"I'm attending a community college. I'm not ready to leave home yet, and my parents can't afford to send me away," I said to him. I saw relief wash over his face. "Were you afraid I would go away and meet some college guy?"

"Pft, no," he replied.

"You did," I smirked, moving my finger in front of his face.

"Okay, yes, I did, but that's because I'm in love with you." His declaration took me by surprise. Nate told me he loved me, but not that he was in love with me. "I know it surprised me too."

I reached up and turned his face to mine as I leaned in and brushed my lips against his.

"Good, because falling in love with someone that doesn't feel the same would suck."

"Best birthday, ever," he said as he kissed me again, deepening the kiss.

New Year's Eve, the Grays had a party, and we all went except my parents. They stayed home as usual. It was your typical gathering, and Lucille being Lucille slipped me a drink. Such an evil influence.

"Lucille," I said.

"Don't be such a party, pooper. It's not like you're going to some random party. Plus, it's New Year's Eve. Live a little," she said as she went to talk to guests.

Nate made his way to me, and I took a sip of the drink. I about gagged. It was horrible. What do they put in this stuff, turpentine? I dumped it out in the sink.

"What's that?" Nate questions me.

"Your mom's idea of a delightful time."

He laughed. "Sounds like ma." He drank his beer.

"I'll stick to pop," I said to him.

"Excellent choice," he complimented me.

It's not like this is my first go-around with alcohol. The party I went to would not be the first time I drank. Lucille would buy wine coolers and give me one, and I was fifteen. It was usually Lucille and me hanging out. Weird, right? A parent giving teen alcohol, that was Lucille for you.

As the countdown began, we counted, and as we rang in the new year, Nate and I rang in with our lips. I could never get enough of his kisses. They were always fabulous.

CHAPTER 23

HOT AND HEAVY

You know how, when you're dating someone, things get a little heated. Well, things got a lot heated between Nate and me. I'm not talking about going all the way, but enough.

Being inexperienced as I was, the first time we did more than a kiss, well, let us say it got hot in his bedroom.

We were lying on his bed, kissing, even though I should work on homework, and I felt him move his hand under my shirt. It landed right on my chest, causing me to gasp against his lips.

He stopped and whirled his hand.

"Sorry," he apologized.

"It's okay. I wasn't expecting it." I sat up and fixed my shirt. He sat up and looked at me.

"We don't have to do anything other than a kiss, you know?"

I took a deep breath and looked at him. "The thing is, I do, but it's a little scary."

"Okay, how about if we take it nice and slow, and any time you feel uncomfortable, tell me to stop?"

I nodded my head and bit my bottom lip.

He looked at me and reached down and dragged my shirt up over my head. Then he took his hands and pulled down my bra straps until he revealed my chest. I watched as he lowered his head and contacted my skin, holy hell.

He cupped my chest as he kissed my skin, letting his tongue glide over it. He worked one, then went to the other side. I let out a small moan when he did that.

He focused on my chest. He made his way down to my waist of my jeans and undid the button, and pulled down the zipper to give him access. The minute he slipped his hand into my pants and under my panties, my breathing hitched.

I moved my legs, giving him better access, then it hit an area that made me groan. He worked his hand and mouth. I couldn't stop my body from moving, causing my heart to speed up and increase my breathing.

Then it happened. Nate crashed his lips to mine as I groaned, and my body shuddered. I grabbed his shirt as he continued, causing me to continue to groan against his lips.

It was an earth-shattering experience. Nate pulled his hand out of my pants, and I let go of his shirt, falling back onto his bed, leaving my chest still exposed.

Oh, my God, that's all I can say.

As I lay there in my blissful state, he lay down next to me and started kissing me again. I couldn't resist his lips. Then I heard a zipper followed by his breathing increasing. I opened an eyelid to see him taking care of business.

My eyes widened. Shit. I didn't know it was that big. Nate reached for my hand, placing it on him, then put his hand on top of mine, guiding me.

Within minutes he found his release and groaned. Ew, it was all sticky as it coated my hand. I pulled my hand away and looked at it. That was so gross.

He lay on his back with himself still exposed with his eyes closed, trying to catch his breath. I leaned over the bed and grabbed the nearest thing I could find so I could wipe off my hand. Then I handed it to him.

He opened his eye and laughed. Taking the clothing piece from me, he cleaned himself off, then tossed it to the hamper in his room.

I pulled down my bra, and he pulled up his boxers to cover himself.

"Did we do what I think we did?" I asked him.

"Yep," he answered.

"Interesting," I responded.

He propped himself up. "Did it bother you?"

"No, it felt weird."

"Trust me; blue balls is not fun." He smiled, and I couldn't help but laugh.

"Do guys do this often?"

"Pretty much. I mean, sometimes you don't have a choice," Nate shrugged.

"Have you done this a lot since we started dating?"

"Yep," he confessed.

"Really?"

"Trust me; it's better than pushing you into something I know you're not ready for yet. Sex is a very private and intimate thing. It's emotional, and a girl's first time is always the hardest," he said.

"I'm afraid I won't be any good at it," I sighed.

"That's why I take my time and take care of you when it happens," he said, playing with my fingers. "Patty, I want it to be special for you. That's why I'm in no rush. Because you only get one first time."

I had to hand it to Nate; he understood these things. I lay down on his chest, and he wrapped his arms around me. I knew in my mind that my first time would excite me, but I also knew that I had been nowhere at that point yet.

The other stuff we did, yes. Sex? No sex can wait.

After that evening, I had so many questions. Curiosity got the best of me.

Nate sat on my bed and paced back and forth, trying to think about what I wanted to ask. I told him I needed to talk to him. He did not understand what I wanted to talk about, but his curiosity peaked.

I finally stopped and looked at him. "So, when we have sex for the first time, does it hurt?"

"Yes," he said.

"And there is blood?"

"Yes, there is," he responded to my question.

"So, pain and blood are what I get to look forward to?" I questioned him, not happy with the thought of it all.

He gave me a look and reached for my hand, pulling me to him. "Relax, Patty; you're overthinking this."

I sat down next to him. "Nate, I'm nervous. Like a very nervous."

He turned to face me. "It's not like we have sex today or tomorrow. It happens when it happens."

"When's that?"

"When you're ready to have sex," he reminded me.

"What if I'm not ready for a long, long time?"

"Then, we wait."

I felt some relief when he said that. Most guys are in a hurry to take that step, but it was different with Nate. He had much patience with me, which I was grateful for with Nate.

Later that evening, after Nate left, Liz stopped by. I opened my door and yanked her into my room. "Well, hi to you, too."

"Sorry, but I need to talk to you," I said, closing my door.

"Yeah, got that when you called me frantic." She looked around. "I thought you were hanging with Nate?"

"He had to go home and help his dad with something," I answered, waving her question off.

"Okay, so what did you want to talk about?"

"Sex," I blurted out.

She raised her eyebrows and took a seat on my bed. She crossed her legs and placed her chin on her fist, and said, "I'm all ears."

I sat down next to her. "Okay, so the other night, Nate and I were kissing, then we did other stuff."

"What other stuff?"

"Like he kissed my chest and placed his hand down my pants. Stuff."

She looked at me. "Go on."

"It was amazing. Then Nate did things to himself and had me put my hand on him."

"You gave him a hand job," she said in a question like a statement.

"Um, I guess," I said, giving her a weird look.

"And?"

"And he said he does that a lot, and this white sticky stuff ended up in my hand, and it was weird and."

She stopped me. "And you gave Nate pleasure."

"Huh?"

She lifted her head and uncrossed her legs, turning to me. "He gave you pleasure, and you gave him pleasure. Patty, when you're with someone, it's not about you. The other person has to enjoy themselves."

"That's the thing; I don't know whether grossed out by it or excited," I said with confusion. "I mean, how was it for you when you first did something like that?"

"It was weird, but after I also knew that it was normal. Then other things happen, and it leads to sex. It's a course of events. Why do you look like you want to puke?"

"Because I want to hurl," I said to her.

"Patty, you need to relax. You're overthinking this way too much. I'm sure Nate does things at your pace and nothing you're uncomfortable with," she reassured me.

"He said the same thing to me." I looked at her. "Did he talk to you?"

"What? No!"

My expression changed. "Nate did!"

"I do not understand what you're talking about," she denied.

"Liar," I accused her.

She looked at me and sighed. "Fine, Nate called me. He had nothing to do with his dad tonight. He wanted to give us some privacy so we could talk," she said to me.

"Great, he's sick of my questions and had to send in reinforcements," I huffed.

"No, he thought you would feel less anxious about things by you talking to me. Patty, it's okay to be nervous, but trust me. It won't last, and it becomes natural," she reassured me.

They were both right. I'm overthinking everything, but it was because this was all new to me. Can't blame someone for feeling this way, can you?

CHAPTER 24

DECISIONS

After being back in school for a few weeks, my work kept calling to know when I was coming back. Scratch that, they demanded to know. My answer was still the same, I didn't know, but that wasn't good enough. I'm sorry, but having a co-worker attack me right before Christmas wasn't something I asked for that evening.

Along with Lucille, Grayson, the guys, and my parents watched me in the Grays living room pace back and forth. I enjoyed working, and I needed the money for school, but I did not feel safe going back to the grocery store.

"Patty, if you don't feel comfortable to go back, don't go," Dad informed me.

I stopped and looked at him. "But I need a job. The school won't pay for itself."

"But you also have a tuition grant and scholarships to help. Plus, your dad and I were talking, and we figure we can both help you with the minor expenses," Mom reassured me.

"But I enjoy working," I pleaded with them.

It was getting us nowhere. Everyone was giving me every reason to quit, and I was countering everybody.

"Might I make a suggestion?" Grayson said to us. We all looked at him. "How about you quit and focus on the rest of your senior year and come fall? You can come work for me?"

"What?"

"That's not a terrible idea," Nate said.

"Jonas works with me, Cayson works in another plant, and I'm trying to get Nathaniel to come for a while now. If you do, he follows," he said, turning his attention to Nate, who rolled his eyes.

"I would, but I have my schedule for the new year and their daily classes. I need an evening job," I said to Grayson.

He rubbed his chin and thought about it. "Okay, how do you feel about cleaning?"

"I mean, I can clean if needed," I suggested.

"Then, after class, you can come and clean the offices for a few hours. Nate can even bring you and stay with you until you finish. That way, it doesn't interfere with school, and you can still earn money," he offered me.

It sounded like a fantastic idea and would help. Plus, Nate would be around, so I wouldn't have to worry about anyone messes with me.

I looked at my parents. "What do you think?"

"Patty, it's up to you. Remember when you came home at sixteen and shoved a work permit in my face. Said either I sign it, or your mom would? I couldn't stop you then, and I can't stop you now," Dad reminded me.

"Yeah, I was ambitious," I agreed with him, tapping my finger to my lips.

"Your dad is right. You've always been ambitious," Mom said in agreement. "Plus, I know I wouldn't worry as much if you were working for people we know."

"Then it's set. Patty works for Grayson and goes to school, and I'm one step closer to having a daughter," Lucille said.

We all looked at her.

"What? Say what you like, but Patty is my daughter one day." She shrugged, getting up.

I had no words for that. We discussed my future and my job situation. Lucille was ranting about me being her daughter. Why do I have a feeling she had something to do with Grayson's offer?

It's Lucille. She always has something to do with my life.

I had decided. I was quitting the grocery store. I spent there all the time coming in when they needed someone. They couldn't be a little understanding of what I went through.

Nate went with me. I needed backup, and he was the best person for that; they didn't want my mom to come with me.

We walked into some yelling. Nate and I looked at each other. That sounded like my mom. When we got into view, we realized it was.

"My daughter has been an exceptional worker, and all you think about is yourselves!" After that, the words went flying. I have never heard my mom drop the F-bomb as much as she did at that moment.

I thought the manager would hurl; he looked pale. People were staring, and the employees stood there in shock as my mother went off on him.

I walked over to them finally and touched my mom's arm. She finally stopped and looked at me. "I wanted to have a few words with this wretched man."

"I see." I turned to him. "Mr. Anderson, I quit."

He looked at me as another woman walked up. "What do you mean you quit?"

I turned to see the store director standing there. "I quit. I don't feel safe coming here, and Mr. Anderson keeps calling my house and harassing me to come back."

"What?" She looked at us, confused.

I turned to him. "I guess you haven't been honest about what you've been doing, have you?"

"Patty, when your mom called and explained what happened, I told her to take as much time as you needed. I did not understand that Richard here has been calling your house."

I took a deep breath. "It's not even that, Pam. A co-worker attacked me. I put my trust in people, and they destroyed it. A guy I thought was decent and nice turned on me. I loved working here and enjoyed the people I worked with, but when I can't feel safe, that's a problem," I said.

"I understand. I hate to lose you because you are one of our best employees," she said to me. "I'll tell you what, if you ever need a recommendation, come see me."

"Thanks, Pam."

She turned to Mr. Anderson. "Come with me, Richard. We need to discuss your future here at the store."

He hung his shoulders low and his head down as he followed behind her. I had a feeling Mr. Anderson's future wasn't looking bright. I felt better than I did.

The three of us walked out of there, knowing that things would change. I could focus on my senior year. I lined up school and a job up in the fall with my parents helping me with the school. Nate and I were doing great.

As for the making out, we kept that to a bare smallest. It was better that way. It stressed me enough as it was. I didn't need the extra stress added to it.

I also couldn't stop thinking about the fact that marriage brought up twice with Nate and me. That made me think about my future with him. I loved Nate and was in love with him, but the question was, would we end up married one day?

The strangest part is when I thought about it. I pictured a little boy running around with Nate chasing after him. The little boy had the same steel-grey eyes and black hair. That made me smile.

If it was any other guy, I wasn't sure, but I saw it with Nate. The scary part was that it made me thrilled.

CHAPTER 25

MY GIRL: A VALENTINE'S DAY CHAPTER

All-day at school, I was feeling excited and anxious. Nate had something planned for Valentine's Day and wouldn't tell me what it was. Ugh, I hate surprises.

Thinking about it was making it hard to concentrate on my classes. All I wanted to do was rush home and find out what it was. The only hint Nate gave me was to wear a dress, fantastic. It's February and snowing. On top of it, it's like fifty below outside and expected to wear a beautiful dress. The man is insane.

After the sixth period, I raced to my locker, tossed my books inside, grabbed my stuff, and left. I needed to find out what Nate had planned. No one would tell me, but they said Lucille helped him. Should I worry?

Once I got home, I ran into the house to get ready. I flung open my door and became stunned. I walked in, and they're all over my room was roses upon roses. I walked into a floral shop. They were unique colors, but there were at least a hundred.

"I guess someone wanted to make sure you had a good Valentine's Day," I heard Mom say.

I turned to her. "When did these come?"

"While you were at school. The delivery guy showed up and said they had a delivery for one Patricia George," she announced.

I turned and looked at them. "The flowers are beautiful."

"Here, this came to you," she said, handing me a card. I took it and opened it.

It was a humor card with Nate's signature, along with a time he was picking me up. I looked at my watch. Crap, I had an hour to get ready. I could do this.

I rushed like a lunatic to get ready. I wore the dress I wore to homecoming. What? Don't judge. It's a beautiful dress.

I finished with a few minutes to spare. I heard a knock on my bedroom door.

"Yeah?"

Mom opened the door and said, "Your date is here."

I smiled at her, grabbing my coat and purse as I walked past her towards the living room.

There he was in a black overcoat, sitting on the couch. I looked at his wrist and noticed he was wearing the ID bracelet I got him. The boy got bonus points for that.

He turned to see me standing there and stood up. I walked over to him. He's dressed in a black suit under the overcoat.

"Ready?"

"Yep," I answered.

He took my coat from me and helped me put it on. I zipped it up, and he waved to my dad, as did I, as we left.

We walked out to his car and got in. He turned and looked at me. "Is that the dress from homecoming?"

I looked down. "Yeah, is it bad?"

"No!" He cleared his throat. "I was hoping you would wear it because you look stunning in it," he said, starting the car. I couldn't help but blush at that.

He drove us to a restaurant, and we got out and walked in. It was elegant. Plus, I noticed it had a dance floor. The hostess showed us to our seat and seated us. I opened the menu and tried to find something I was familiar with to eat.

"You look confused," he said.

"I am. I don't understand any of the terminologies on this menu," I said to Nate.

He smiled and pointed to something. "Order that."

"What is it?"

"Steak, trust me, I learned the hard way when I came here with my dad for a business meeting. It was around the time he thought I would follow in his footsteps."

"Which you chose not to do since you work on cars?" I said.

"I enjoy working on cars. I always have. The business world isn't for me."

"So, if you had a chance to, let's say, own a business, what kind of business would you own?" I said to him. I was curious about what he would say.

"I guess a manufacturing business with parts — something I understand. Now, Jonas, he's good at the business aspect. Cayson is great with computers. I'm good with knowing what is a valuable part is and what is defective," he said to me.

The server came over, and we ordered and continued our discussion.

"So, if that's the case, why don't you tell your dad this?"

"Because he wants us to take over his company when he's ready and to do jobs we don't want to do. I would rather be happier than being rich," he said to me. I couldn't disagree.

Money is okay, but if you don't understand the value behind it, then all it is a piece of paper.

"Now, we didn't come here to talk about jobs. We came here to enjoy a nice Valentine's Day date," he said with a smile.

The server brought our food, and we ate. I had to admit the steak was excellent.

"Nate, you know how you said on your birthday about marriage," I asked him as I ate.

"Yeah?"

"I was thinking, if one day you asked me, I would say yes." I looked up from my plate at him. He looked at me and gulped hard. I diverted my eyes back to my plate. "But, I figured that would be off distance."

I heard him set his silverware down and stand up. I lifted my head and looked at him. He took a step towards me and got down on one knee. Whoa, I said future, not now!

He reached into his pocket and pulled out a black velvet box. He opened it and there stood in the light was a ring, but not an engagement ring.

"Patricia, I know when the time is right, I ask for your hand, but I want to make you a promise that one day, I ask you to be my wife. From the moment we kissed, I knew where my heart belonged. Watching you grow up and become the woman you are today has been amazing. Those late-night talks we would have on your picnic table made me realize something. You are my best friend. They say you fall in love with your best friend, and they were right. Will you accept my promise ring?"

I looked at him and got off my chair, then knelt in front of him. "Always," I answered. I wrapped my arms around his neck and kissed him; then he pulled me into a hug. The restaurant cheered, and a few women smacked their guys for not being as romantic, but I didn't care.

Nate was everything I had hoped for and more. He took the ring out of the box and slid it onto my finger. It was beautiful.

We stood back up and sat back into our seats, finishing our dinner. The music started, and people went out onto the dance floor. He stood up and held out his hand. "Want to dance?"

"Thought you would never ask," I smiled. I took Nate's hand, and he led me to the dance floor. He spun me around, then pulled me to him, and we started dancing.

As we glided across the dance floor, he looked at me as he held me tight. "I'm wondering something."

"What's that?" I asked.

"If you need a date for homecoming, why didn't you ask me? I would have taken you," he said to me.

"I wasn't planning to go, then your brother asked me out of the blue."

He gave me a look. "You didn't ask him?"

"No, I was going to stay home, but then he knocked on my door and asked me," I said.

"He told me you asked him when I asked him about it."

I looked at him. "Yeah, I'm sure he asked me. Do I look like the person who approaches a guy to have them take me to dance?" I said as a matter of fact.

He looked up and sighed.

"What?"

"I knew she was behind all this," he said, mumbling.

"Who?"

"My ma, she has been plotting and planning for years to get us together," he grumbled.

I looked at him and smiled. "Lucille might have plotted and planned, but we got together because we wanted to. Do you regret any of it?"

He looked at me and smiled. "No, can't say that I do because everything with you has been amazing."

I moved my arms up and wrapped them around his neck. "I feel the same."

After the slow song ended, Nate spun me out, and we started dancing in sync. People moved out of the way as we danced to a fast song. We kept our eyes on each other as we danced side by side and then in front of each other. His footwork was impressive.

He was even great at keeping up with me as we danced. People watched us as we danced, then did a clap, clap, clap as he grabbed me and spun me around with him. We finished with him dipping me. People clapped, and he lifted me and bowed.

"Next show is in thirty minutes, folks," he grinned. He led me back to the table.

We sat back down and said, "Where did you learn how to dance like that?"

"Ma taught me along with Jonas and Cayson," he shrugged.

"That makes sense because Jonas can dance," I said to him.

"You should see us at weddings. All the guys do this crazy routine. It's a Gray thing," he said to me.

We enjoyed the rest of our evening. One thing is for sure. I needed to see this dance routine the Grays do together. One day, I will.

CHAPTER 26

I SWEAR LUCILLE IS CRAZY

Valentine's Day was fantastic. Nate made everything memorable. I could not ask for a better day. But like most things, there's always some craziness in the mix, which usually involves Lucille.

Now, she's usually crazy with her antics, but this time took the cake. I pulled up from school to see cops and ambulances in the Gray driveway. What in the hell?

I walked over and to see what the deal was. Then I saw Nate sitting in the back of an ambulance with an ice pack, a busted lip, and a bloody nose.

Cayson was in the back of the cop car, and Jonas was not looking too hot. I walked over. "What happened?"

"Ma happened," Nate answered.

"What did she do?" I asked him.

"Jonas and Cayson got into a slight altercation, and well ma incited the situation. Things got out of hand, and when I came home, all hell broke loose. Now they're taking Cayson to the police station and Jonas to the hospital," he explained.

I had no words. That was insane. I walked around and found Lucille, who was talking to a police officer, "Lucille."

She turned to me. "Hey, Patty," she greeted me.

"What is going on here?"

"The boys had a minor scuffle," she said.

"You incited a riot," I said.

"Well, Cayson went after Jonas, and I told Jonas to beat his ass," she said.

"And Nate?"

"Nate should have stayed out of it," she said as a matter of fact.

"How can he stay out of it when he walks into a mess?"

"Patty, my boys had always been rough. That is nothing new," she said to me.

"I don't even have words," I said, walking away. How can a parent instigate a fight between their kids? That is beyond me, but this is Lucille we are talking about here. She has always been bat shit crazy.

I walked over to Nate, and they finished him up, and he got out of the ambulance's back. I gave him a concerned look and reached up, touching his face. He hissed at the pain.

"Your mother is crazy," I told him.

"What else is new?" He shrugged.

Then Grayson pulled up. Shit.

He got out of his truck, spotted Cayson in the back of the cop car, saw Nate, and spotted Lucille. He walked past us, and Nate whispered, "This isn't good."

Then the yelling started, "What the hell is wrong with you?"

"Well, Cayson shouldn't have attacked his brother," she yelled back.

"That's it! He's out! I want him and his stuff out of this house!"

"Grayson!"

"No, Lucille! That boy has no direction and a short fuse! I'm sick of it!" he declared.

I looked at Nate. "Did your dad kick your brother out of the house?"

He sighed as he said, "Yeah."

I looked at Cayson as he sat there in the back of the cop car with his head hung low. The police pulled out and left with him while the ambulance took Jonas to the hospital.

I stood there in shock. Never in a million years would I ever think this would happen. Nate might have had a temper, but Cayson had a short fuse. It would forever change life at the Gray house.

Grayson refused to allow Lucille to bail out Cayson or anyone else, and even if he's bailed out, he could not come home. Grayson was firm about it. I couldn't help but feel bad for Cayson.

They released Jonas the next day. Cayson did a number on him. He broke his nose and a few ribs, leaving him with a ton of bruises.

Nate explained to me they got into an argument, and it got out of control. He never told me what the fight was about, and I didn't ask.

The few times I went over there, it was a distinct atmosphere. We didn't stay long, and Nate ended up spending more time at my house.

I walked into my room and handed him a glass of pop as he sat on my bed with his back against the wall. I crawled up and sat next to him.

"Have you spoken to Cayson?"

"Yeah, he's staying with my aunt and uncle until he can find a place," he said. "It's not the same since that day. I mean, ma and Dad act like everything is okay, but Jonas won't talk about it, and Cayson is angry," he said.

"All families have issues," I said to him.

"Yeah, but our issues seem to have grown over the years." He turned and looked at me. "Patty, I love my family, but sometimes it gets too much."

I could see where Nate was coming from with his family.

"So, what are you going to do?"

"I could move out, but then I wouldn't be across the street from you." He turned and looked at me. "If I go, I want you to come with me. I can handle leaving, but I can't handle leaving you."

I looked at him; then, I said something unexpected. "Okay."

"What?" He looked at me.

"I'm eighteen. I graduate this year and in school, along with working for your dad. If you can wait until after I graduate, then we'll go," I said to him.

"Patty, you know, your parents won't allow you to move in with me without us married," he said to me.

"Then I guess we'll get married."

"Whoa!" He scooted off the bed and looked at me. "Do you know what you're saying?"

I got off the bed and stood up.

"Listen to me, Nate. I've had much time to think about this. Yes, it disappoints my parents, but they'll get over it. Plus, we can make this work," I said to him, taking his hands in mine.

That was it for me. I didn't want anyone but Nate. He was everything to me, but seeing what was happening with his family made my heartache. I knew my parents wouldn't be happy, but it didn't matter. What mattered to me was him.

He wrapped his arms around me. "Are you sure about this?"

"With every heartbeat," I said to him. He held me tight, and I held him back.

With that settled, we waited until after I graduated and made things official. Lucille was rubbing off on me. I had never thought of doing something this crazy before, but as she said, live a little.

Things were about to get even crazier.

CHAPTER 27

MYRTLE BEACH FOR SPRING BREAK? SURE, WHY NOT?

For spring break, Lucille offered to take Liz and me with her to Myrtle Beach. Nate came along, as did Jonas and Danny. Cayson was still angry with his parents and brother, so he definitely wouldn't be there. Sucks. I would have loved to have him there.

We drove down with Lucille and the girls in one car and the boys in another.

"Lucille?"

"Yes, hun?"

"It's nothing." I couldn't bring myself to ask her about Cayson.

"You want to know about Cayson, don't you?"

My head snapped, looking at her. Was this woman a mind reader or something?

She glanced at me. "Nate told me you were asking about him."

"I didn't want to ask if it was a sore subject."

"It's not, but Cayson needed to learn a lesson," she explained to me. "His temper has gotten the best of him. He and Jonas got into a stupid argument, and Cayson threw the first punch. I love my boys, but sometimes I'm tired of them acting like petty bitches."

I heard Liz snickered in the back seat.

"Patty, one day, when you have kids, you understand what it means to play a referee."

"Have you spoken to Cayson since then?"

"I'm still his mother, but Grayson meant what he said. We do not allow Cayson back home, period."

"I thought mothers were to defend their children?" I questioned her.

"To a point, but you have to remember your husband stay after they leave home," she said finally. God, I hope it's not like when I have kids. I guess it depends on how you parent them.

We pulled up to a rental and got out of the car. We grabbed our bags and went inside, finding our room. Liz and I took one bedroom while the boys and Lucille got their bedrooms. I didn't mind; It gave us time to talk.

"Girls? You hungry?" Lucille yelled up to us.

"Yeah," we yelled back.

"I fix lunch; then we can hit the beach!"

"Okay," we both yelled.

I set my bag on the bed and opened it. Liz set her purse on the other bed and turned to me, "Spill."

"About what?" I said, digging into my bag for a suit.

"About what's going on with you and Nate. Do you think this week is the week that you finally, you know?"

"What? No, why would you think?"

"Well, because you both have been dating since November, and it is now April," she said to me.

I gave her a look, "I don't think there is any time frame on when it happens. Everyone is in such a rush. Like Nate says, you only get a one-first time," I replied to her.

I didn't have the heart to tell her we were getting married and leaving once I graduated. It was nothing against anyone, but we chose this path for us.

We changed into our swimsuits with shorts over the bottoms, walking downstairs. We had lunch, then hit the beach. I removed my shorts, and Nate did a double-take. He picked up a towel and walked over and covered me.

"Nate? What are you doing?"

"I don't need guys staring at my fiancé!" My eyes widened, and I tried to shush him, and the rest yelled, "What?"

Nate, you idiot!

We turned and looked at them as they stared at us in shock.

"And when is this so-called wedding?" Lucille asked him with her hands on her hips.

"We were going to elope after Patty graduates," he said. I smacked him. "Ow," he mouthed.

"Do Dad and Mom know?" Danny asked me.

"Well, no," I said.

"Oh boy," he said, sighing.

Lucille walked over to us. "You want to get married? Fine, but no elopement. We have a wedding at the house," she said as a matter of fact.

We looked at her, and she turned and walked away. Jonas looked at us. "Did you think you could run off and elope without ma knowing?" Then he started laughing.

"Wait until we get home. Lucille tells Mom," Danny said, walking away, and Liz shook her head, following behind him.

I smacked Nate. "What the hell, woman?"

"You have an enormous mouth, Nathaniel Mark Gray!"

"So what?" He pulled me to him. "We're getting married, and I can't wait."

"You're still an idiot." I rolled my eyes at him.

"Yeah, well, I'm your idiot," he said, kissing me.

We walked into the house after spending the day at the beach and found Lucille on the phone. She held out the phone at me. "Your mother would like a word." Shit.

I took the phone and answered, "Hi, Mom." I didn't get a word in edgewise. There was a lot of yelling and cursing, followed by Mom telling me she and Lucille would plan the wedding. That went better than expected.

The rest of the spring break went fine. Knowing I was getting married in two months was a little terrifying — scratch that. It was frightening.

I was sitting on the beach looking out at the water, watching the waves crash upon the shore. The sunset illuminated the sky with orange and red. It was breathtaking and beautiful.

Nate walked over and took a seat next to me.

"I thought I would find you out here," he said as he wrapped his arms around his knees.

"Yeah, I was thinking. How we went from point A to point D?" I said to him.

"Simple, because we know this is right."

"Is it? I mean, we started dating in November, and now we're getting married? Doesn't it scare you?" I asked him with a concerned tone.

"Not being with you scares me more," he said as he grabbed my hand. Then he pulled my promise ring off.

"Nate, what are you doing?"

"Replacing this with the right ring," he said as he pulled another ring out of his pocket. He got on his knees in front of me.

"Pat, this may seem like it's moving fast, but it isn't. We have known each other our entire lives. From the time we shared late-night talks, our first kiss with each other, to our first date, and everything else. There is no one I would rather share those moments with than with you. You're it for me. I couldn't imagine my life with anyone but you. So, I have to put the right ring on this time," he said, slipping an engagement ring on my finger in place of the promise ring.

I looked at him and leaned forward, placing my hands on his face and kissing him.

Life becomes unexpected. While most people wait a while, we have expected our entire lifetime to be together. Some people would say this is fast, but it took us eighteen years to get here.

We've both seen each other at our best and worst. It's that boy and girl, sitting on the picnic table. We had those late-night chats about everything and nothing at all.

He sat down, pulled me between his legs, and wrapped his arms around me as we watched the sunset.

He leaned in and whispered, "Patricia Gray has a delicate ring to it."

"Yeah, it does," I smiled.

The rest of the spring break went well, and we headed for home. The minute we got home, I went inside to face the firing squad, and boy did I meet it alone, Nate that coward.

My parents weren't happy but accepted it. Mom reasoned, if they fought against it, we would run off and elope. Nate had to deal with Grayson. Poor Nate, it was nice knowing you. I will bring flowers to your funeral.

Grayson wasn't happy but dealt with it. They said it was because he liked me a lot. I didn't know whether I'm so glad or terrified.

That also meant Nate had to look for a place for us. We couldn't very well live with our parents while married. That would be weird.

Whatever happened from here on out, I knew one thing: I would graduate and get my degree. There was no way I would throw that away after all the hard work I put into it.

CHAPTER 28

AND THE COUNTDOWN BEGINS

I pulled up to the front of the house, getting out of the car after school. I met with Nate, placing his hand over my mouth and shushing me. He waved me to follow him.

"Where are we going?" I asked in a whisper.

"Far from here, our moms are in full wedding mode," he whispered.

"Enough said," I whispered and got into the car.

He pulled out the driveway, alerting Lucille and Mom that we were leaving.

"Are they leaving?" She asked.

"It looks like it," Mom replied to her.

"Figures."

We drove over to Liz's hiding out. It was the one place we wouldn't have to deal with wedding planning with our mothers. Plus, I needed to work on schoolwork, and I couldn't do that when people bombard me with questions.

Liz and I sat in her room, working on homework while Nate laid on her bed. It was beautiful and peaceful until we heard pounding on the door. Liz's mom opened the door, and before we knew it, Jonas and Danny walked into the room.

We all looked up at them. "Thanks for leaving us with the lunatics," Jonas snapped at Nate, who chuckled.

"I swear Mom has lost her damn mind," Danny said, sitting down next to Liz.

"Hence why we're here, and they are there," I said to him.

"Yeah, but you can't hide forever," he said to me.

"I can try," I smirked.

"A few more weeks and this is over with," Nate said to him.

"Yeah, but did you also forget we have finals and prom along with graduation to get through," Liz reminded him.

"Shit," he remarked.

"Which means we have to find a dress, and you two have to find a tux?" She told them.

"Do we have to?" They whined.

"Yes, it's our senior prom," she said to both of them. I laughed. They forgot we were seniors and still in high school.

We finished our homework, then ordered a pizza and watched a movie. As we watched the movie, I leaned over and whispered to Nate, "Did your mom invite Cayson to the wedding?"

"I don't know," he whispered back.

"I hope so," I whispered to him, and he gave me a look.

I thought to myself. It wasn't right if Cayson didn't get invited. No matter what happened, he should be there since his brother is getting married. Guess I ask Mom about it.

Nate took me home, and I walked into the house. Mom was waiting up, reading as usual. I sat down in the chair.

"How was your evening?" She asked me.

"Peaceful," I sighed. Mom laughed. "Mom, can I ask you something?"

"Sure, hun," she said.

"Is Cayson invited to the wedding?"

"I don't believe so. Why?"

"I wondered. Night," I told her as I got up and went to my room. I got ready for bed. I thought to myself, they may not welcome him in that house, but he sure in the hell welcomed to our wedding. If not, there is a change in plans.

I stopped over at Lucille's after school to talk about whom they invited to the wedding. I needed to make sure Cayson was there.

I knocked on the door, and she answered, "Come inside, Patty."

I walked through the door and into the kitchen.

"Lucille, I'll get right to the point. Is Cayson invited to the wedding?" I refused to beat around the bush on this.

She looked at me. "Yes, but I don't think Cayson comes." She said.

I looked at her. "If I can get Cayson to come, will you promise me Grayson is on his best behavior?"

"I can try, but it's Grayson."

"Promise me," I said.

She looked at me. "I promise. You take care of Cayson, and I'll take care of Grayson." She gave me a smile and a wink. Okay, then. Now all I have to do is persuade Cayson to come to the wedding. Let's hope he isn't too stubborn about this.

She gave me the address of where he was staying, and I drove over there. It wasn't too far from where I lived. I pulled into the driveway and got out, making my way to the door. I knocked on the screen door.

A woman answered it and explained to her who I was, and she welcomed me inside. I walked in, and she called for Cayson at the bottom of the steps. I heard a door open and then footsteps.

He strolled down the steps with his hands in his pockets.

"Patty? What are you doing here?"

"I came to invite you to our wedding," I said to him. He arched an eyebrow and looked at me, then at his aunt. Something tells me someone has been lying.

We sat in the living room, the three of us.

"So, let me get this straight. You and my brother are getting married right after you graduate?"

"Yep," I answered.

"And my parents approve of this?" He arched an eyebrow at me.

"Well, it was this or eloping," I said.

He let out a low whistle.

"Cayson, I want you to come to the wedding."

"My dad won't allow it. He won't even allow me to come over," he said, shaking his head.

"Which reminds me, what exactly did you and Jonas argue about?"

"It was stupid. Jonas was ribbing me like he always does, but I let my anger get the best of me. I hit him; he hit me, then it turned into the mess that happened. The worst part was hearing my ma tell him to kick my ass, which pissed me off even more. Nate tried to break it up while arguing with me, and it escalated from there," he explained.

"Yeah, Nate's not thrilled about it," I mentioned to him.

"Makes two of us," he sighed.

"Look, I'm asking you to come. Nate should have all his brothers there. Whatever is going on with you and Jonas, put aside for him," I pleaded with him.

"That's the thing, Jonas, and I already talked. We're fine. It's my parents that can't seem to put it behind them," he said with a shrug.

"Don't worry about them. I got my plans," I smirked.

If I have learned anything about being around, Lucille is to beat her at her own damn game. It was one game I intended to win.

I gave Cayson the day and time to show up. Since it was my wedding, I deserve to have people there that I want there, even if Nate may have reservations about it. Oh yeah, I didn't tell him my surprise. That should be fun.

CHAPTER 29

PROM

With Prom coming up, Nate and Danny had to rent tuxes for the night. Ha! That teaches them to date high school girls.

Liz and I went shopping for dresses. I wanted something simple and easy to manage. She tried to look hot. Yeah, we have two distinct ways of looking at things.

As we scoured the racks looking for a dress, I heard the most annoying voice out there. Do you know that voice that sounds like nails across the chalkboard? Yep, that would be the one.

"Well, well, well, look who it is if it isn't the trash girl herself."

I turned to see Tricia with another girl, "I see you're still recycling the same insults that Brian uses. Must be great not being original," I smirked.

She glanced down and saw the ring. She grabbed my hand and yanked it to her. "Is that an engagement ring?" She stuttered on the engagement part of her sentence.

I yanked my hand away. "Yes, not that it's any of your business." I crossed my arms across my chest.

"How? How can a guy that works in a garage afford a ring like that?"

"Simple, he saved for it, and it doesn't matter. Ring or no ring, I would have said yes. I would rather have a guy that gets his hands dirty from honest work. Then a guy that sponges off his rich girlfriend," I snapped. I was so over with this conversation. It was the same bullshit every time I saw those two.

Liz and I left that shop and went to another shop. All I wanted to do was buy a dress, not explain how my boyfriend paid for a ring.

As we looked for dresses, Liz looked at me. "You know people are talking."

"About what?" I moved a hanger over, listening to the metal hit against each other.

"The reason you two are getting married is that you're pregnant," she snickered.

"Unless it's an immaculate conception, I don't think so," I said as I looked for a dress.

"It doesn't bother you that people are talking?" She asked me.

"No, let them talk. I know the truth, and Nate knows the truth. In a few weeks, none of this matter. We'll have graduated, and I'm married."

"What about school?"

"What about it?"

"Well, do you plan on still going to school?"

"Yeah, I didn't come this far not to get a degree. Plus, I have a job lined up, and Nate is looking for a place for us."

She looked at me. "What?"

"Patty, I'm not trying to squash your dreams. Once you get married, everything changes if kids enter the picture," she stated.

"Liz, I get that, but I know this is the right choice for me." I gave her a soft smile. I saw a future, and Nate was part of it. I never pictured a guy in my future. A career? Yes, I did. Kids? Yes, kids too. A guy? That would be a big fat no.

I guess it was because I didn't see him. I wasn't ready to see him, but I see him now.

After finding a dress and shoes, we went home to get ready. Yep, I'm a big procrastinator. Imagine my wedding day, which reminds me I haven't even got my dress for that. Is a bed sheet is acceptable?

We got ready, and Mom knocked on my door. "You girls almost ready?"

"Mom, beauty takes time," I said to the door.

"Beauty? Woman, if you aren't ready in five minutes, we aren't going?" Leave it to Nate to ruin a moment. I swear, would this be how he is when we're married?

"I swear that man is impatient," I huffed.

"So, explain to me how he's so patient with waiting, but yet impatient?" She asked me.

"Beats me. Nate is a strange person," I said.

We finished up and walked out of the room. Danny and Nate were waiting on us. They pinned a corsage on each of us, and my dad took photos. Then we were off.

We arrived at Prom and got out of Nate's car. I took his arm, and he walked with me into the banquet hall. He leaned over. "You look beautiful tonight."

"Well, you look handsome yourself," I smiled. Nate smiled back at me, and we walked into the banquet hall. We found our seats, the four of us. It was cool.

They served food, and there was dancing, and there was the announcement of Prom King and Queen. Guess who got it?

Brian got King, but Queen surprised us all. They announced my name as Queen, which didn't sit well with Tricia. The weirdest part, I don't even know why I got picked.

The King and Queen had to dance together, fantastic.

Brian took my hand and placed his other on my waist, and I put my other hand on his shoulder. They played the song for the King and Queen.

"You know I don't like this any more than you," he blurted.

"Doubt it. Let's get through this dance, and you can get back to your date," I huffed.

We danced, and he mentions, "So, I heard you're getting married."

"Yeah, so?"

"Congrats," he shrugged.

I looked at him. "Thanks, even though I know you don't mean it," I blurted.

"Look, I don't want to fight anymore. In a few weeks, we graduate and won't have to see each other anymore," Brian said to me.

"Fine, but keep your dog away from me," I said to him.

We finished our dance and moved away from him as I could, running towards Nate. The minute I reached him, I took his hand and led him to the dance floor. I wanted to dance with my date and fiancé.

"So, what was that all about?" He asked me.

"Brian is trying to put the past behind us, but I don't trust him. The only plus side is in two weeks. I never have to see him again." I couldn't help but smile.

"This is true, but you know what else is true?"

"What's that?"

"I get to wake up next to my wife," he smiled, and I couldn't help but blush. I still couldn't believe we were getting married right after graduation. It was surreal.

Nate secured a place for us but wouldn't tell me anything about it. He said it was a surprise. That had me a minor worried.

Let's see a backyard wedding and a home I have never seen before. What could go wrong?

We danced for a while, then the four left and went back to my house. Nate pulled into the back, and we got out of the car. He walked over to the picnic table and took a seat, patting the spot next to him.

I walked over and took a seat next to him, as did Danny and Liz.

"Is this what you two used to do all the time?" She asked us.

"Yep," we both said.

"That's cool," she said.

As we sat there, he looked at me. "I've decided." I looked at him, confused. "I've taken my dad up on his offer."

"What? No, Nate, you love working on cars," I said to him.

"Exactly, which is why a part division opened up at the plant. I'll start at the bottom and work my way up. It's more money and benefits. Plus, there's a chance I get to see you more often when you work for him," he said with a smile and a wink.

"Are you sure this would be what you want to do?" I asked him.

He took my hand and placed his in it and said, "For our future? Yes, Patty, in a few weeks, you're my wife and family. I want to take care of you."

I smiled at him. Nate didn't make this decision based on one thing but made it because of us. I knew no matter what, things would be okay for us. Well, at least I hope they are.

CHAPTER 30

FINALS AND GRADUATION: THE END OF ONE THING AND THE START OF ANOTHER

I was so focused on studying for my finals. I forgot one insignificant thing, my wedding dress. I didn't forget; I got sidetracked from it. I was to pick one out and order it, in case it needed alterations, oops.

My finals were this week. Graduation was next week, and well, the wedding was the weekend following graduation. Trust me; this won't end well, considering that was the only thing I needed to do.

I studied, and Nate helped me by quizzing me on each subject. I was ready to finish high school once and for all. Next up was college. The eye on the prize, the eye on the title, is what I had.

We had finals three days in a row. So we could have a break and study for the other ones. Then, after finals, there was practice for graduation. If they have to tell you how to walk up and get your diploma, you are a certifiable idiot.

Some of our classmates needed extra instructions, along with no drinking and drugs. It should be common sense, but none of this is familiar, and there is no sense.

Can't I graduate now?

Graduation finally arrived, and I pulled on my gown, zipping it up. I took my mortarboard and pinned it on my head, taking one last look in the mirror.

"Wow."

I turned to see Nate standing there in a pair of black slacks and a button-up shirt.

"You look beautiful," he complimented me.

I smiled at him and held out my arms. "But I'm wearing a tent."

"Yeah, but you can make a burlap sack look good," he smirked. I couldn't help but laugh. Then he pulled something out behind his back.

I looked to see him holding a dozen red roses. "Nate! They're beautiful," I exclaimed.

"So are you," he said, leaning over and kissing me on the lips. "Ready?"

"Let's get this show on the road," I said as I walked past him carrying the roses.

I don't know why, but I felt nervous. I mean, agitated. I've been looking forward to this for four years, and now it's happening.

Graduation, a time to reflect on four years of high school. Accomplishments you have made, the friends you have made, and the life you created only moved on to a new chapter. It was scary.

We pulled up and got out of the car. I found Liz, and we talked. Then we're told to take our seats.

Graduation started. I sat there remembering this past year and everything that happened. It seemed like a lifetime ago, but it was only this past year.

At the beginning of the senior year, it started with me liking someone else, and Nate and I were not getting along. Then things shifted. It happened when Brian made the comments he did about the Gray boys. He had destroyed whatever illusion I had of him, and Nate replaced it, showing me not all guys are bad.

I thought about our talks and how he made me laugh and care about what I had to say. We still think about our trip to the apple orchard, Halloween night, the party. Our first kiss on our first date. I knew when I fell in love with him only to have him fall in love with me back.

The cuddles we shared, the laughs, the conversations, and I turned and looked at Nate. He looked back at me and smiled. There was no mistake, I was in love with Nathaniel Gray, and in three days, I would become his wife. Then it hit me. Shit.

Liz looked at me and did a double-take. "You look like you'll hurl," she whispered.

"I am."

"Why?"

"I didn't get my dress." I winced.

"What?" She yelled.

Everyone turned and looked at us.

"What? Haven't you all seen two girls discussing their periods? Now turn around," she said to everyone, getting weird looks from them. Kill me now.

She leaned over and said, "We need to go now."

"What about Graduation?"

"Screw graduation. We graduated. It is formalities. If your mom and Lucille find out you didn't get your dress, you won't have to worry about graduation. We will attend your funeral," she stated to me.

"Good point," I said as we both got up and ran to the car, causing everyone to turn and watch us leave.

Liz started the car and threw it into the drive and peeled out of there. Forget graduation and the dress. I would die in the way she was driving.

She pulled up in front of a bridal shop, bringing the car to a screeching halt.

"Are you going to sit there? Come on," she yelled at me, running into the bridal shop. I got out and ran in after her. We were still in our cap and gown, causing people to stop and stare at us.

She ran to the counter and laid on the bell. A woman came out and removed her hand from the sound.

"Can I help you?" She spoke in a snooty tone.

"We need a dress, stat," she said.

"For whom?"

"Her," she thumbed at me. She looked at us. "Look, lady, she is getting married in three days. She shows up in anything other than a wedding dress. Her mother and soon-to-be mother-in-law will hurt her," Liz said.

"I'm sorry. I can't help you," the woman said in a snobbish tone and walked away.

"Bitch!" Liz yelled.

Great, not only did I miss graduation, but I can't get a damn dress. I was dead.

"Um, excuse me, I couldn't help but overhear you needed a dress," a woman said.

"Are you a sales lady for here?" I asked, pointing at the bridal shop.

"Oh, god, no," she laughed. "But I have a dress shop. We could find you something suitable for your wedding," she said, waving us to follow her. So we did.

We followed her to a dress shop, and we walked in. It had dresses upon dresses. I saw nothing in white, which didn't sit well with me.

"Now, I may have the perfect dress for you." She smiled and walked towards the back. She returned a few minutes later, carrying a box. "Here, go try it on," she said, handing me a box.

I took it from her; then walked towards the changing rooms. I closed the curtain and set the box down. I opened it, and my jaw dropped. I reached down and pulled the dress out. Lace and beads adorned it, and it was stunning.

I changed out of my clothes and put them on—the dress fit. I looked in the mirror.

It was what I had imagined as my wedding dress. I opened the curtain and walked out. Liz and the woman's eyes widened, and jaws dropped.

"Wow!"

"Beautiful," the shop owner complimented.

"I can't believe it fits," I said, turning around.

"That dress is amazing," Liz said.

"I can't believe someone would want to give this away," I said to her.

"People part with things. Then that item finds a new home," she said with a smile.

"I'll change, then pay for it," I said as I went back to the changing rooms. I removed the dress, placed it back into the box, and put it back on my clothes. As I put the lid on the table, there was a note attached to the white box.

I opened it and read it;

I had a feeling you would forget something. So I made sure I covered this. Love your grease monkey.

I shook my head and laughed—that figure. I picked up the box, carrying it out to the counter, then set it down and looked at the woman. "Do I even want to know?"

She smiled at me. "Let's say someone loves you very much." I smiled and picked up the box, and walked away.

How he even knew, I did not know. But what I knew is this confirmed my decision.

CHAPTER 31

WEDDING DAZE

The night before the wedding, us girls hung out at Lucille's while the guys were out doing God knows what.

It was weird to have my mom, Lucille, Liz, and Nate's Aunts there. We all talked and ate pizza.

"I still can't believe you're getting married tomorrow," Liz said to me.

"Neither can I, but I can't wait," I said. "Nate turned out to be amazing." They sat around and listened to me.

"We went from neighbors to friends to more. He is my best friend."

"What made you decide Nate was the one, Patty?" One of his Aunts said to me.

"When he kissed me for the first time. It was my eighteenth birthday, and we argued, but the minute he kissed me, it was like it didn't matter anymore. It's like forces were pushing us together," I said to Nate's aunt.

"More like the force of Lucille pushing you together," another aunt said, which made us laugh.

"I always knew it meant them to be together, even though they were both as stubborn as jackasses," Lucille said.

"Gee, thanks," I said, rolling my eyes. We laughed more and talked most of the night. While the guys had a guy's night, they also practiced something for the wedding.

"Ready?" Grayson said to them.

They nodded and stepped in sync with each other. The weird part was Cayson's included. After I talked to Nate and told him what I did, he had a chat with his parents. They relented.

Threatening elopement gets them every time.

I woke the next morning and looked at the clock. In a few hours, I would be Mrs. Nathaniel Gray. It was surreal.

I heard a knock at my door, and it opened. "You won't sleep all day, will you?"

"No," I yawned and sat up. I got up and stretched. I had to get my butt in gear so I could get ready. Liz would be here in an hour to help me.

I had breakfast, then showered. Liz showed up and was already ready. She went into my room and did my hair and makeup. Mom got ready and then helped me get into my dress. Lucille stopped by to help.

When they finished, I turned and looked at them, "Well?"

"Sweetheart, you're beautiful," Mom said to me, which made me smile.

There was a knock at the door. "Everyone decent?"

"Yes, dad!"

He opened the door and took one look at me and smiled; I smiled back.

"We better go. Grayson said the groom looks like he's ready to pass out," he said to us.

They walked out of my room, and I walked over to him. "My baby is getting married." A tear fell down his cheek.

"I know, Dad, I know." I leaned over and kissed him on the cheek. My eyelashes brushed against his skin, giving him butterfly kisses. He held out his arm, and I took it. He led me to the Gray house, and we walked in through the front door.

We were getting situated; Before we started, someone placed a bouquet of red roses in my hand. I looked at them and smiled. Only one person would do this.

We walked to the family room and the patio door. The music started, and Jonas met Liz, escorting her, and Cayson met with a cousin escorting her. I stood there with my dad. When they cued us, we stepped through the doorway and started walking up the aisle way towards Nate. He stood there, grinning from ear to ear.

When we reached him, Dad handed him my hand and said, "Take excellent care of her, Nate."

"Always," he said as he took my hand and held it, intertwining our fingers.

We turned, and the minister started. Every so often, I glanced up at Nate, and he glanced down at me. As we said our vows, we slipped our wedding rings onto each other's fingers.

"By the power invested in me, in the State of Michigan. I now pronounce you, husband and wife," the minister announced. "You may now kiss your bride."

Nate spun me around and dipped me, kissing me as my arm hung down with the bouquet, and someone snapped a picture. That would be my dad.

He lifted me and placed his hands on each side of my face, and said, "I love you, Mrs. Gray."

"I love you, Mr. Gray." He pulled me into another kiss, and everyone clapped.

After the wedding, we all sat and ate with the bridal party talking.

"Well, Patty, who would ever think the neighbor girl would finally get my big brother to settle down?" Jonas said, placing his hand on Nate's shoulder.

"I guess it takes a majestic woman," I shot back.

"Touché," he chuckled.

"Attention, everyone," Liz announced, clanking her glass and standing. "It is now time for the best man and maid of honor speeches, and I am going first," she said, causing everyone to laugh.

"I have known Patty forever, and I could not ask for a better best friend. Even with her neurotic tendencies, I love her like a sister. Nate, I am handing over my best friend to you. Take wonderful care of her. To Nate and Patty!" Everyone raised their glasses and toasted us.

Then Jonas went, "Well, Peppermint Patty, I may have gone to homecoming with you, but Nate was the one to win your hand. Nate is my big brother, and I watched their friendship blossom over the years. I'm glad they finally got together, or ma would never leave Cayson and me alone. To Nate and Patty!"

People toasted us again, then Nate stood up. "Thank you both for that, even though I sometimes wonder about you both." We all laughed. "I never thought I'm here, married to that junior girl, kitty-corner from me, but I'm glad. She is not only my wife but my best friend, and I couldn't think of a better person for that. I love you, Patricia Gray." He leaned over and kissed me with a collective aww from everyone.

Then it was my turn; I stood up and said, "To be honest, I had a crush on Nate for years, then one day, he became a pain in the ass." Everyone laughed. "But over time, as things changed between us, I realized I couldn't imagine my life without him. I didn't fall in love with the neighborhood boy, but I fell in love with my best friend. I love you, Nathaniel Gray." I leaned over and kissed him.

After our toast, we cut the cake, then the dancing began. Nate and I danced first. He took me in his arms and held me close. We danced together, and Nate held me tight. I knew as he held me; he would never let me fall.

I looked at him. "Thank you for the dress."

"I couldn't let my future wife deal with ma's wrath, now could I?" I giggled. We danced together, and held me close to him, giving me kisses every so often.

Nate was my future, and I could not have asked for someone better than him.

After we danced, they had everyone clear the dance floor. Grayson and the guys walked onto it, and other family members. The DJ started a song.

Then they started. Nate and his family's shoes hit the floor with a thud, and then they moved in sync with each other. I stood there in amazement. I watched as they flipped each other. It was all in step. Then Liz pushed me onto the floor. I saw their actions and followed along until Nate grabbed me, and we did our dance together.

I never had so much fun as I did at that moment. We all clapped and stepped and finished with Nate dipping me. Then everyone joined in.

Our wedding may have planned, but it turned out perfect. Sometimes you have to live a little.

CHAPTER 32

THE WEDDING NIGHT

After a while, Nate grabbed my hand and led me away to the car. We got into the car, and he drove to our next destination, the honeymoon suite.

We checked in. When we got to the room, Nate picked me up in his arms and opened the door, carrying me over the threshold —such a romantic.

He set me down, and I looked around. They filled the room with red roses. It was amazing. I turned to him. "Did you do this?"

"I had help," he smirked.

He pulled me to him and kissed me. As he left my lips, he trailed kisses down my neck. He reached behind me and undid my dress, letting it fall to the ground, leaving me exposed in my underwear.

I looked up at him as he undid his shirt.

"I'm a little nervous," I whispered.

He pulled off his shirt and undid his pants, letting them fall to the ground. He stepped out of them and walked towards me. "It's okay."

I gulped as he looked at me with a hungry look in his eyes. As he walked towards me, I backed up against the bed and fell backward onto it. He climbed on top and hovered over me.

My breathing hitched as he kissed me. I reached up as he continued to kiss me. He pulled my bra off, followed by my panties, then pushed off his boxers. He reached over and grabbed something. I watched him as he opened a foil packet and pulled out the contents.

I dropped my head onto the bed. Once he finished, he pushed my legs apart and said, "Relax."

I nodded, and he lowered himself down on me as I closed my eyes. Then I felt it at my entrance. I reached up and grabbed his shoulders, preparing myself. He pushed himself inside of me, causing me to gasp at the intrusion. Then he stopped.

I caught my breath as did he, and then he pulled out, then slammed inside of me. Holy hell, that hurt! I cried. He whispered in my ear, soothing words, reassuring me it was only temporary. I nodded and told him to keep going, so he did, over and over. It took a minute, but the pain finally subsided as my body started moving with his.

It was hard for me. I did not understand what I was doing. Nate lifted me until I was sitting on his lap and thrust inside of me. My breathing hitched, and I felt my muscles tighten. Then he said, "Baby, it's okay. Let it go."

"I can't, Nate," I breathed.

"You can. Please, baby. Give in and let it go."

Then it happened; I groaned. I moved my hips on Nate's lap as I felt immense pleasure course through my body. That, in return, caused him to groan low into my ear, finding his release.

Once our bodies came down from the intense pleasure, he laid me back down on the bed and kissed me. He put on top of me, stroking my cheek.

"That was amazing," he said to me.

"That was insane," I responded to him, and he chuckled.

"Why did you hold back?"

"It scared me," I said, looking at him.

"Why?"

"Because it's scary knowing someone has that much control over your body," I said.

"It is, but it's also amazing." He leaned down and kissed me.

He pulled out and got off of me, walking to the bathroom, naked. I looked to see his butt. Damn, he has a cute butt. He returned shortly with a washcloth, cleaning me up. It was a little messy.

Then he tossed the washcloth and climbed into bed, lying down next to me. I turned onto my stomach, and he looked at me.

"How do you feel?"

"A little sore," I commented as I lay there.

"It'll be better."

"God, I hope so because that freaking hurt," I said. He laughed.

He pulled me to him and made love to me again. I had to admit this time was so much better. We fell asleep with him, cuddle up behind me. We interlocked our hands with our wedding rings with each other.

I fell asleep next to my husband, and I could not be happier.

I awoke to something poking me. I opened an eye to see Nate cuddling up at me moving his hips against me. I gave him a look. "Really?"

"Yep," he answered.

Then he pulled me under him and threw the covers over our heads.

"Nate!"

"Shh, it'll be quick, and I'll get you breakfast."

"Well, in that case."

I sat in bed in a robe as I heard the door opened and Nate walked in, wheeling in a cart of food. I climbed off the hotel bed and walked over to it. He removed the lids, revealing breakfast.

"Told you I would bring you breakfast," he said, kissing me.

"Yes, you did. I'm starving."

"Good, now eat up, woman. I have something to show you in a few hours."

I shrugged, taking a plate and fork while sitting on the bed. We had breakfast together and talked. It was so surreal to know that I graduated from high school, eighteen, and am now married.

I still couldn't wrap my head around it or last night. I felt like I was still in a daze.

We talked about new things and kids being one of them. Both of us felt we could wait before starting a family. I had a school and worked to deal with it in the fall, and he was starting a recent job. So until then, it looks like we're buying stock in a condom factory.

I didn't mind. We needed to get acquainted as husband and wife because they say the first year is usually the hardest. God, I hope not.

After we ate, we took a shower and got acquainted again and again. Nate was right. Once you get past the first time, sex is much more fun. We got dressed. When he set up the room, he brought our bags already with a change of clothes, since we didn't bring any bags.

We gathered up all our things and checked out of the room. We walked out to the car and set our stuff in the back seat, climbing in.

He looked at me. "Ready?"

I looked at him and smiled. "Ready."

With that, we were off. Where was Nate taking me?

CHAPTER 33

WELCOME HOME MRS. GRAY

"Your eyes close?" Nate asked.

"Yes, for the hundredth time. I don't know why you felt the need to carry me," I spoke, sounding annoyed.

"Because that's the fun in it," he chuckled.

Finally, we stopped, and he set me down. He leaned down to my ear. "Ready?"

"Yep," I replied.

"Open your eyes," he said.

I opened my eyes and stood there looking at a house that's not finished.

"It's nice," I said.

He walked in front of me. "I got a good deal on it. Dad and my brothers help me fix it up, and it's our dream home. Hun, what do you think?" He asked me.

I smiled at him. I didn't want to dash his dream, but this was where we would live? Oh, boy, this would be something.

He grabbed my hand and led me to the front door. Forget that. He dragged me to the front door, opened it up, and showed me around. The house needed much work.

Between electrical, plumbing, and drywall, I would say this would be an exciting place to live. No wonder Nate got it dirt cheap. It was a dump. I hope he knows what he's doing.

I woke up to banging. I looked around to see Nate gone. Then I heard a saw. What in the world?

I got out of bed and stuck my head out the window to see Cayson on a ladder. "Sorry, Patty," Cayson apologized.

"Cayson, what are you doing?"

"I guess Nate didn't tell you we were stopping by," he smirked.

"Ugh!" I pulled my head in and stomped out of the room and down the stairs.

"Hey, Peppermint Patty!" Jonas yelled.

I took a deep breath. "Where is my husband?"

"Kitchen," he nodded towards the kitchen.

I walked to the kitchen, passed other guys, and found Nate and Grayson working on the kitchen lights.

"Nathaniel!"

He turned and walked over to me, closing the distance between us. "Morning, baby," he greeted me as he kissed me.

"Don't morning me!" I glared at him. "What is going on here?"

"We're working on the house," he said.

"Now? You couldn't wait?" I exclaimed.

"If we wait, it won't get done quicker," Grayson interjected.

I gave him a look. "Thanks, Grayson, but this is between my husband and me." Grayson backed off. I looked at Nate. "Fine, but next time, tell me when everyone is planning on being here. I know to expect them," I demanded and turned, walking away.

I may sound like a spoiled brat, but can you blame me? Imagine waking up to people banging and pounding away, not knowing they were coming. Yeah, you wouldn't be too happy either.

Knowing I would have people always in and out of my house, I became accustomed to them. Plus, with Nate changing jobs and doing the recent job, he was working on the house if he wasn't at work. I pitched in and help. I got good with a mud knife.

That is how we spent the first three months of our married life. It wasn't bad, but it was much work.

One day I walked into the bedroom and collapsed on the bed. I was beyond exhausted, and no, I wasn't pregnant.

He walked to the door and chuckled at me, laying face down on the bed. He walked over and climbed onto the bed next to me.

"For eighteen, I figure you would have more stamina," he snickered.

I turned my head and groaned. Then I propped myself up.

"I didn't realize how much work this is," I said to him.

"Working on houses is always a colossal job. Wonderful thing, my family and I are good with our hands," he said, holding up his hand and wiggling his fingers.

"How long do you think it is until it's finished? It's not that I don't mind having a bunch of families invade our home. It would be nice to have some on one time with my husband," I said, reaching up and pulling his lips to mine.

"Soon, I hope," he said as he wrapped his arms around me, pulling me close to him. As he was about to kiss me, we heard something break. We looked at each other and scrambled off of the bed. We ran downstairs to see a branch break the living room window.

"I can fix that." I looked at him and placed my head in my palm. We live in the money pit. It would be a long first year.

Nate boarded up the living room window. The tree by the window came down. Cayson brought another window over and installed it.

While I watched him work on the window, the lights started flickering. Now what? Then I heard a surge of electricity and all the power went out.

"My bad," Jonas yelled.

"Looks like Jonas wired something wrong," Cayson snickered.

"I'm thinking they wired Jonas wrong," I replied to him, making him chuckle.

Then I heard the front door open, and someone yelled, "What happened to the electricity?" Well, Nate's home.

He walked into the living room. "Pat?"

I looked at him. "Jonas happened."

"Great, fanfuckingtastic," he huffed. Remember how I said Nate had a temper. Well, this was one time his anger showed. "Jonas! I'll kick your ass!" He walked away.

"Jonas better run," Cayson suggested.

"Why?"

"Because when Nate's mad, he throws stuff. Hell, he threw a wrench at my head one time," he said to me. My eyes widened, and I ran after Nate.

I found him ready to beat Jonas and decided that the only logical thing to do was jump on his back.

"Pat!"

"Nate," I said.

"What are you doing?"

"Giving my husband attention," I said, wrapping my body around his back.

He sighed and looked at Jonas. "You're lucky. I love my wife."

"Yeah, I'm sure she loves it when you love her," he said, wiggling his eyebrows.

"Jonas?" I said.

"Yeah?"

"Don't," I advised him.

He shrugged, and Nate walked around with me on his back until he set me down. He turned to me. "This was not how I imagined this would be."

I looked at him and saw the disappointment in his eyes. The enthusiasm left, and now it felt like a chore to him. I reached up and touched his face. "Babe, it's okay. Life isn't perfect, and neither is this house, but with enough hard work, it's amazing."

"You think so?"

I lowered my hand and reached for his. "I know so. Trust me; when everything is said and done, we appreciate this so much more." I smiled at him, and he pulled me to him as he wrapped his arms around me.

"That's if I don't kill my brothers first." I giggled, and then the lights came back on. We looked around.

"See," I said. Then the lights went back off, "Or not."

"My bad," Jonas yelled.

Nate rolled his eyes, and I laughed. Yes, it would be a lot of work, but it would be worth it when we finished. I was sure of it.

CHAPTER 34

SETTLING INTO MARRIED LIFE

As Nate, Grayson, Jonas, and Cayson worked in the house, I started school and my recent job. College differed from high school. I went from six classes to three over four days, with two courses on two days and one course on the other two days. It was weird to me.

Then I started work at Grayson's company meeting with HR to fill out paperwork and shown around. I would clean the offices and bathrooms. It wasn't exactly what I wanted, but I needed the money.

With the house renovations happening, we ate out a lot. I would be so happy to have a kitchen, fridge, and stove for use. Eating out is okay, but I miss home-cooked meals. Thank God we had my mom and Lucille because that's where we went when we ate out.

Nate and I settled into married life. To be honest, it felt like it did before, with a few minor differences, I.e., sex. Other than that, it suited us both.

As the days turned into weeks and the weeks turned into months, we moved towards the holidays. I had also finished my first semester of school, aced it, and became used to my job at the plant.

I couldn't wait for the holidays. I had set aside some money to buy everyone a little something. It's nothing too fancy, a little something for everyone. I had Christmas bulbs engraved for each person with their names on them. I thought it was cute.

Nate was running a little behind the night I was to pick them up, picking up something for the house. I waited for him in Grayson's office, knowing no one would bother me in there.

I had told no one, but a guy in another division wouldn't leave me alone. He was always making some inappropriate comments towards me and trying to touch me. I told him if he didn't stop, I would go to Grayson. The guy was creepy as it was, plus I know my husband's temper. It would piss off Nate.

I sat in Grayson's chair, waiting on Nate, looking at a magazine when I heard the door open and closed.

"It's about time," I said, thinking it was Nate, except it wasn't. I looked up to see Gerald from shipping standing in front of the door. I stood up. "Grayson isn't here."

"Oh, I know. Everyone has left." He shrugged when I heard a click. Shit.

"What do you want, Gerald?" My tone was icy.

"What I've wanted since the first day? A date," he smirked.

"I already told you, I'm married."

"Yeah, yeah to Nate," he said, dismissing me. "It's funny. He doesn't act like he's married when he's here, so I figured you both have some kind of arrangement."

I gave him a look and licked my lips, trying to figure his game. Nate would never cheat on me, let alone flirt with another woman. Grayson would beat his ass if he did. Then he was trying to upset me by making these ridiculous accusations.

"No, we don't have an arrangement, and you don't know my husband very well," I said. I ran my hand along the edge of Grayson's desk. He stepped closer to me and felt around under the top of Grayson's office.

Then my finger felt it, a button. I let it lingered as he moves closer to me, then when he was face to face with me, I pressed it. Not once, but a few times. Thank God Nate told me about the silent alarm Grayson had installed.

"Then I guess I have to change your mind, now won't I?" He spoke to me before lunging at me. I picked up a heavy book and whacked him across the head with it. When you grow up with the Gray boys, you learn to defend yourself.

He grabbed his head and stumbled back as I ran to the door. I fumbled with the locks as he got to his feet and staggered towards me. Finally, I got the door open, and there stood Nate and Grayson.

My eyes widened as Nate looked past me to see Gerald rubbing his head. I looked at Nate. "He thought we had some arrangement, so I whacked him across the head with a book."

"What kind of arrangement?" Nate said to me with a stern look.

"That we sleep with other people and that you have been messing around on me, so he thought I would do the same," I said. Does it not dawn on anyone who tried to attack me, and he's still breathing?

Nate gave me a look and rolled his eyes. "First, I work with all guys, and I have no interest in them, and second, why is he even in here?"

"How should I know? He came in here and locked the door while I was waiting for you to pick me up. You're late!"

"Sorry, there was a problem with the counters," he exclaimed.

"Gerald here has been harassing me. He thought tonight would be a magnificent night to follow through with his harassment," I said to him.

Nate did a double-take. "What? Why didn't you say anything?"

"Because I didn't want people to think I was asking for favoritism. Because my father-in-law is the owner," I said.

He gave me a look. "Pat, you need to speak up about these things. It's not about who you're related to here. It's whether it's right," he said to me as he lifted my chin. Then he turned to Gerald and said, "You're fired," then turned back to me.

"This is insane! You can't do this!" Gerald protested.

Grayson looked at him. "He can, and he did. Now get out before I call the cops," he ordered him. Gerald stormed by us, mumbling something under his breath. I never understand why anyone would think that's okay? I would like one job where some douche didn't attack me. That would be nice.

"When we get home, we are having a nice long talk about you are staying quiet about problems with other people," he said. He wrapped an arm around me and pulled me close.

"Okay, but first, we need to make a stop," I said to him.

"Where?"

"To pick up the Christmas gifts, I ordered. They close in thirty minutes," I said, grabbing his hand and dragging him out of there.

"Yes, dear," he sighed, earning a chuckle from Grayson.

After that night, Nate and I had a long talk about expressing if we had any problems. I showed I didn't appreciate him being late, and he expressed himself by doing other things. I won't even go there.

Grayson and Nate talked. They decided it would be better if I worked with Nate dealing with the shipping situation. Gerald had been making many mistakes that were costing the company much money. Since I was going to school for business, this worked out.

The holidays were chaotic when Jonas met a girl and brought her home for Christmas. It didn't go too well.

Karen seemed nice but a little standoffish to everyone. She was close to Jonas's age, and I don't think she knew how to take the Grays. But then again, unless you grew up with them, no one knew how to make them.

I watched her fidget when she was around people and broke the ice.

"Karen, is it?"

She looked at me, wide-eyed, "Y-yes?"

"I'm Patty, Nate's wife," I said, introducing myself.

She looked me up and down, then exclaimed, "But you're so, so."

"Young?"

"Yes," she answered.

"I turned nineteen," I smiled, and her jaw dropped in shock. "But I have known the Grays all my life. I grew up with them."

"Oh," she whispered.

"It's okay; they're an interesting bunch."

"I don't think his mom likes me very much," she said with a pained expression.

"Okay, this is what you need to know. Lucille is crazy. Simple, but she loves her boys. She has a weird way of showing it. Grayson is a little harder to figure out, but he's very nice, and then there is Nate and Cayson. Nate has a temper, and Cayson doesn't care what people think. But Jonas, he's the sweetest guy you ever meet," I explained to her.

Nate walked over to us, and I introduced them. Lucille called me over to her, and Nate stood there with Karen.

"Pat seems very nice," she said to him.

He looked at her and arched an eyebrow. "Patty is amazing. I couldn't have asked for a better wife. My parents adore her," he said to her.

"Oh," Karen mumbled.

"Word of advice." She looked at him. "Pat is the one you want as an ally." He walked away from her, heading over to his mom and me.

I had a feeling; It was going to a long and hard road for Karen, but if Jonas cares about her, they would be fine. I guess time might tell.

We made it through the holidays. I also found out my brother and Liz got engaged on Christmas, figures.

Well, they are happy because Liz can be a handful. At least we'll be sisters.

We settled into married life, and I couldn't be happier. Well, that's until things took a turn for us.

CHAPTER 35

TIME TO TAKE A BREAK AND HAVE FUN

School, work, and house renovations are almost complete. Nate decided we needed to have a break. I was finishing up with my second semester, and he got some time off for us from work. The boys had the renovations under control. We headed down to Nashville, Tennessee, for a long weekend.

Nate had rented a place for us to get away and relax. Plus, I wanted to take in some sights.

Once we arrived, he pulled up to a log cabin. I got out of the car and looked at it. "You know, if you wanted to go to a log cabin, we could have gone to your family's cabin up north," I said to him.

"Yeah, well, it's cold, plus this puts hundreds of miles between them and us," he grinned, and I laughed.

He opens the door, and we walked inside. We set our bags down, and he closed the door. I looked around, and the next I knew, he picked me up and carried me to the bedroom. "Nate!"

"Live a little woman!"

He closed the door, and things got a little crazy. So crazy, someone forgot to wear their raincoat. He rolled off of me as we caught our breaths, and I asked, "Did you wear protection?"

"Um, well," he lifted the sheet, looked down, and then dropped the cloth, "funny thing."

I looked at him. "What?"

He looked at me. "I sort of forgot to put it on." He winced.

"What?" I sat up; then, he sat up. "Nate, you know I'm not taking anything!"

"But you had your woman thing," he said.

"But it doesn't mean I won't get pregnant. After that, we ovulate dipshit!"

"Oh," Nate said.

Ugh, he had one job to do. Wear the damn raincoat! I ran my hands through my hair in frustration. I love my husband, but sometimes he doesn't think with the right head.

"Pat, look at me." I turned to face him. "Look, if it happens, it happens."

"Nate, I still have the school to finish, not to mention having to work to pay for school," I said to him.

"We'll figure it out, and I'm sure our parents help us if we need it. Plus, I'm making good money at the plant," he reassured me.

"A baby? Are we even ready?"

"I am," he smiled. He reached over and pulled me to him. "Look at me. I love you, Patricia Gray, and I can't wait to start a family with you."

I looked at him and sighed. "Well, if it happens, then I guess we deal with it."

He placed his hands on my face and kissed me again. Then we all know what happened next. Nate thought the practice would make perfect. It scared me, shitless.

We took in the sights and explored Nashville, but I had babies on the brain. Everywhere I looked, I saw babies.

I pictured what it would be for Nate to be chasing a little one around. Could I be that wife that took away a chance for her husband to have a family of their own? Was I selfish? I know I worked so hard to go to school, but Nate has done a lot for me.

I sat on the bed and sighed. Nate came out of the bathroom and looked at me. "Pat? What's wrong, baby?"

I looked at him. "I don't want to be selfish." Then I cried.

He walked over, closing the distance between us, and sat down next to me. "Baby, you are the most unselfish person I know. What got into you?"

"I keep thinking about school and work, and what if I end up pregnant?" I babbled. I looked at him. "Nate, I don't want to take away your right to be a father."

He looked at me. "Is this what this is about, Hun? Pat, look at me. If we end up having a baby, I'll make sure you get to finish school. Okay?"

I nodded and sniffled.

"See? Compromise," he smiled.

I threw my arms around his neck and hugged him. He was the most fantastic person I had met.

Our trip ended, and we went back home. At the moment, we weren't even sure I was pregnant since it was too early to tell. I guess we would have to wait to find out.

Waiting is the hardest part.

I started the third semester and worked. I became preoccupied with everything that I forgot to check one important detail.

I was checking the calendar to see when the next shipment came in and looked at the date. It was April 20. We went to Tennessee on March 3. Did I have my period? When was the last time I had a period?

I started counting in my head. I stopped a week before we left, and I should have started twenty-eight days later. I counted the day from the first day of my last period on the calendar. Then it hit me. I'm late.

Nate walked in. "Patty, I need the dates of the shipments."

"Nate, I'm late."

"Yes, I know. You were to come back ten minutes ago," Nate said, looking at the schedule.

"No, I mean, I'm late," I said, grabbing his arm and looking at him.

He looked at me. "I know."

"Not the shipping schedule, you idiot. I'm late as I'm late, late," I said, giving him a look.

"Oh," his head snapped up. "Oh!" He looked around. "Ah, what do we do?"

"Get a test," I suggested.

"Right. Be right back," Nate said, running out of the door. I sat down in the desk chair and took a deep breath. Oh, dear.

Nate returned twenty minutes later, carrying a brown paper bag. He handed it to me, and I went right to the bathroom. I never thought I would take a pregnancy test at work. I figure it would be at home, alone.

I waited as I heard knocking on the door. "Sorry busy!" There was knocking at the door. "I said I was busy!"

"Betty Crocker, it's me."

I opened the door, grabbed Nate's arm, and yanked him inside. I closed the door and locked it.

"Well," he asked me.

"I haven't gotten the result yet," I said to him.

"How long do these tests take?"

"How should I know? It's the first time I ever took one," I said.

Then we heard a knock at the door. "Patty, is everything okay?"

I looked at Nate. "It's your dad," I mouthed.

"I know," he mouthed back with a look.

"Oh yeah! I'm taking care of a little something!"

"Well, when you see my son, tell him I need the totals on those shipments."

"Sure thing, Grayson!"

We heard his footsteps walk away, and we finally looked at the test.

CHAPTER 36

SURPRISE?

We stared at the positive test. I took another one to make sure, and sure enough; it was positive, oh boy.

I needed to sit down. I lowered the lid on the toilet and sat down. "I'm pregnant?"

"Well, tests don't lie," he said.

I couldn't tell if I was in shock or surprised. I don't think either of us could, considering Nate kept asking me if I was okay, over and over.

A baby? Oh boy, I thought as I sat there, not knowing what to think.

After our initial surprise of finding out I was pregnant, we kept it quiet. We wanted confirmation from the doctor. I wanted to get past the first trimester. There's always that possibility of losing it, and I didn't want to think about it.

Although hiding, it was easier said than done. When you're always sick and avoiding your family, they suspected something is up.

We confirmed with the doctor, and I was due in December. Our time in Nashville was a success, figures.

I also showed at three months, which meant having to wear baggy clothes. I was looking like a homeless person.

Once we got past the first trimester, we told our families. The only problem was that we walked into a mess in the form of Jonas.

We heard yelling between Grayson, Lucille, and Jonas, oh dear.

We walked in, and Nate yelled, "Hey! What's going on here?"

"Your brother knocked up his girlfriend," Grayson growled. That caused a surprised look on our faces.

"I told ma and Dad that Karen offered to raise the baby on her own, but I told her no. I refuse not to be a part of my child's life," Jonas said as a matter of fact.

"How far along is she?" Nate asked him.

"Two months," he said. "Why?"

"Nothing," he mumbled. It was so not the time to tell them about us.

"Excuse me," I said as I walked away and left their house, heading over to my parents.

"What's wrong with Patty?" Lucille asked Nate.

He gave her a look, and she looked at him. "No," she said, shocked.

Nate sighed and narrowed his lips.

"Excuse me," Nate said, leaving. He walked over and found me sitting on the picnic table outback. He walked over and took a seat next to me. "I thought I would find you here."

"Simpler times," I sighed.

He reached over and grabbed my hand. "It's okay. At some point, we tell them."

"Patty? I thought I heard voices back here," Mom said.

"Hey, mom," I greeted her.

"What's wrong?"

Nate and I looked at each other and then at her, "Is Dad home?"

"Yeah, he's watching TV."

I stood up and pulled down my shirt. And that's when Mom saw it.

"Come on, let's talk," she said, and I walked towards her with Nate following behind. We told my parents the news. They were happy for us.

Then there was a knock at the door. Mom answered it, and in walked Grayson and Lucille. We looked at them as we sat on the couch.

"You boys sure like to do things together, don't you?" Lucille asked Nate.

"The difference is, I'm married," he smirked.

"How far along?" Grayson asked.

"Four months," I answered.

He looked at Lucille. "Well, you wanted grandbabies."

"I guess I did," she said with a smile curling upon her lips.

From then on, it was smooth sailing for us, for Jonas not so much. He and Karen eloped them, moving into an apartment together. Jonas was always the guy to do the right thing. I know deep down he loved Karen, but it happened so fast. They had their difficulties, but don't all couples?

As for Nate and me, pregnancy was a trip. I would get some weird ass cravings and sex, well that was even better than before. Let's say my hormones went into overdrive. I felt bad because I kind of wore him out.

But I loved the way it felt to feel the baby kick and move.

I was lying in bed, reading a magazine, and Nate looked down to see my belly move.

"What is that?"

"The baby," I said, flipping the page.

"What's it doing?"

"Moving," I flipped another page.

He reached over and laid his hand on my belly, then it kicked, "Whoa!"

I smiled. "Amazing, isn't it?"

"It's fantastic," he smiled back. He rubbed my belly and said, "We should pick out a name."

"I know, but I was thinking of waiting until it's born since we don't know what we're having."

He looked at me. "Only because you refuse to find out."

"Hey! I want surprised."

"You hate surprises."

"So?"

He gave me a look.

I rolled my eyes. "Okay fine. I found out what we're having. Happy?"

"I knew it! You little sneak!" He got up and pointed at me.

"I couldn't help it! I had to know!" I spoke.

"Yeah, well, so did I," he shrugged.

"You didn't?"

"I did," he smirked.

"We are terrible people; you know that?" I said to him.

"Why?"

"Because we told everyone we didn't want to know," I said to him.

"Eh, they'll get over it," he said, waving at me. He laid back down and looked at me. "A boy?"

"Yep," I answered.

"I can't believe we are having a little boy," he said, twisting his wedding ring around his finger.

"Which reminds me, what are we going to name him?" I asked him.

"Let's do something different," he said to me.

I gave him a look, and he grinned. I know, I smiled. Oh boy, I knew that look.

It wasn't long before I was ready to pop. We got through most of the holidays except Christmas. I had a feeling our little guy would not wait, and boy, I was right.

He appeared before Christmas. Labor was interesting. Let's be honest. It hurt like a bitch, and I almost crushed Nate's hand. After many, many, many hours, he finally arrived.

They handed him to me, swaddled up in a blanket, and I looked at him. He looked like Nate. He was beautiful.

I handed him to Nate, and he held him. Looking at Nate, holding our son was the best feeling in the world.

"Wow, I'm a father," he said in awe. "Well, little guy, your mommy did an amazing job of bringing you into this world."

The baby let out a squeak, and Nate sat down on the side of the bed with me. I leaned over and looked at both of them—my guys. I could not love them more than I did at that moment.

Everyone came to visit and hold the baby.

"Well, what did you two decide for a name for my grandson?" Lucille asked us. We looked at each other and smiled.

CHAPTER 37

HERE COMES NASHVILLE AKA NASH

"Nashville?" They all exclaimed.

"Well, Nashville Nathaniel Gray, but Nash for short," I told them.

"Why Nashville?" Mom asked me.

"Because it's where he's conceived," I said.

Yep, Nash would kill us when he got older, but I didn't care. His name suited him.

After Nash came along, Nate and I decided it would better if I stayed home with him. I would go to school in the evening, so one of us was back with him at all times.

Nash kept us busy for sure as he started crawling then walking. I had to chase down a toddler, all the while exhausted most of the time. I so needed sleep.

Thank God it was the weekend, and I had no classes. Nate walked in and looked at the house. "Um, Betty Crocker?"

"Yes, grease monkey," I said, looking at him from the couch.

"Is there a reason our house looks like a tornado hit?"

I pointed to Nash.

"Never mind." He walked in and picked up Nash and walked over and took a seat next to me. "You look exhausted."

"I am," I yawned.

"What did you two do today?"

"Well, I cleaned, Nash made a mess, took a pregnancy test, and then we took a nap," I said.

"Wait. Back up."

"I cleaned."

"After that," he said, giving me a look.

I sighed. "Okay, fine. I took a damn test."

"And?"

"I have a doctor's appointment this week," I said to him.

"Another one?"

"Well, when two people love each other," I said.

"Yes, I know how a baby gets made, smart ass. Remember, I was there?"

"You were, but your raincoat wasn't." I shot back.

"That isn't true. I wore one; it broke." He shrugged, and I smacked him.

"Thanks for giving me the heads up," I said to him.

Then we heard the doorbell. Nate stood up with Nash. "Come on, Nash. Mommy is moody when she's pregnant," he said to Nash, who giggled. I shook my head and rolled my eyes.

Jonas and Karen walked in with Jason, whom we called Jace for short. He was two months younger than Nash. They were coming over for a BBQ, as was everyone else.

"Why does Patty look like she's ready to rip your head off?" He asked Nate.

"The raincoat broke," Nate mentioned.

"Damn, son!"

"And I didn't tell her," he added. Jonas chuckled. "What's so funny?"

"Makes two of us," he said, chuckling.

"You know, ma and Dad will have a field day with us?"

"What else is new? Cayson is the smart one out of us," he shrugged.

While the boys talked, Karen and I spoke while Nash and Jace played together.

People arrived, and we had a full house. It was crazy. When we told Grayson and Lucille, we were expecting again along with Jonas and Karen. Let's say they had a few choice words. I won't repeat it because it wasn't pretty. Eh, what can you do?

Nate invited a few people from work, including their kids. We were standing out back when we saw Cayson take some poor girl's plate from her. Then we saw her tackle him and retaking the plate.

"Damn," Jonas said.

"Who is that?" Nate asked.

"That is Franco's daughter, Dominique," Grayson said.

"Franco from receiving?" Nate asked him.

"Yep," Grayson answered.

"Woo boy," he said, letting out a whistle.

We found out later Dominique was 100 percent Italian, and no one touched her food. Poor Cayson, He did it to get her attention. Wrong move on his part.

Everyone had fun at the BBQ and left. I was ready for everyone to go because it tired me. Plus, if the doctor confirmed I was pregnant, this baby would give me a run for my money. I never remember being this tired with Nash.

The doctor confirmed it. Baby number 2 would be here in February. Why can my kids come when the weather is warm is beyond me?

I was an emotional wreck with baby number 2. We decided on his name when we watched TV, and Richard Nixon came on the tv on the history channel. When we said Richard, nothing, but when we mentioned Nixon, he kicked up a storm.

Yep, we were having another boy. Good lord, I am being overrun with boys in my home. I need some girls to balance it out.

This pregnancy was rough. If I wasn't an emotional wreck, I was temperamental. My freaking hormones were going crazy, and poor Nate had to deal with them. Well, he should be careful with his raincoat the next time.

When the day came, Nate was more than ecstatic to have me delivered. He would get a break. Well, Nixon had other plans. He cried a lot.

I had a feeling he would be my temperamental child in the home. I noticed that when Nash and Nixon were together, Nixon was calmer. I had a feeling those two would be close.

While we were dealing with two boys, Jonas was also dealing with two boys of his own. He named his second son Jamison, but we called him Jaime for short. He was as temperamental as Nixon. It must be in February.

As for Cayson, he won over Dominique, and they started dating with them marrying. I loved Dominique. She was funny and could hold her own with Cayson. Must be the Italian in her.

Life is crazy, but as Lucille said, live a little.

CHAPTER 38

DAMN SON, DID YOU FORGET YOUR RAINCOAT?

Life somewhat calmed down, except for one minor problem. Nate and I didn't exactly calm down.

Nixon was around six months old when you guess it. I found out I was expecting again. Not only was I expecting, but Cayson and Dominique were too. Though Nate and I made an excellent team. I couldn't have asked for a better partner. Damn, that was quick.

Breaking the news to our parents was even better.

"Damn, son, did you forget your raincoat again?" Lucille asked him.

"I swear those things are defective," he mumbled, rolling his eyes.

"And thus, I got snipped," Jonas whispered to him, causing Nate's temper to flair and smack him upside the head.

"Nathaniel, Mark!"

He looked at me. "He deserved it!"

"We have little eyes watching us," I said, pointing to the boys.

"Shit," Nate remarked.

"Shit," Nash repeated.

"No! No shit," I exclaimed.

"Shit. Shit. Shit," Nash repeated.

"Well, the kid has a colorful vocabulary," Grayson said.

I facepalmed myself; I only have us to blame.

"Am I getting a granddaughter this time? Because I want to buy dresses," Lucille said to us.

"Ask jackrabbit here," I said, pointing at Nate.

"Me," Nate exclaimed.

"Well, you're the one that determines the sex unless all your little swimmers are boys," I shot back.

"God, I hope so, because it gets you both off my back," he grumbled.

I shook my head.

"So, when is the recent arrival?" Grayson asked.

"May," we both said.

Finally, a warm month to have a baby, thank God.

This pregnancy went better than the last one, but I was more significant than the previous two. I didn't think this was normal, and neither did Nate.

We would also find out the sex. We were both praying it was a girl.

At my ultrasound, the doctor looked, and our eyes widened when we saw the screen.

"Twins?" We both yelled.

"Looks that way," the doctor smiled. Nate passed out. I leaned over and looked at him while shaking my head—an enormous baby.

"Since my husband is taking a siesta, what are we having?" I asked her.

She started laughing. "Sorry to say Mrs. Gray, but it seems you have boys," she said, pointing to the minor member between their legs. Swell, more boys. I give up.

Nate finally came to, and when I told him, he had to sit down. Most guys would be happy to have sons, but with this family, boys ran rampant. It turned out Cayson and Dominique were to have not one boy but three. Cayson said three was enough and got snipped.

I couldn't blame him. Nate still refused. That's when I got on the pill after the twins. At least one of us needed to be safe.

I waddled into the bedroom after getting Nash and Nixon settled into bed. I lowered myself onto the bed while Nate was reading a baby book of names.

"The boys all settled?"

"Yep, after five bedtime stories later," I sighed.

He set his book down and helped me. Being pregnant with twins was rough. Imagine being an animal and carrying a litter. That's what it felt like to me.

He helped me get settled, then crawled next to me.

"Any luck?" I asked, pointing to the book.

"Nope, nothing is standing out to me."

"Well, we can't refer to them as a baby boy a, and baby boy b. We have to come up with some kind of name."

"Well, do you have any suggestions?" He asked with a slight annoyance to his tone.

"Well, I have been reading a book call The Notebook by Nicholas Sparks, and the guy named Noah."

"Noah?"

I looked at him. "Yeah, I thought we could name one, Noah Grayson."

He thought about it and said, "Okay, I can work with that. What about the other baby?"

I thought about it then said, "What about after his daddy?"

"But, we name Nash after me."

"Yes, his middle name, but I'm talking a junior, as in Nathaniel Mark Gray, Jr. We could call him Nathan," I suggested.

He looked at me and said, "We have their names." He smirked, and I rolled my eyes. Leave it to Nate to state the obvious.

"I guess someone bought the house next to us," he mentioned.

"Good, the boys will make a friend. Although Nixon has separation anxiety issues from Nash," I said to him.

"I'm sure Nixon grow out of it," Nate reassured me.

"I hope so because the minute Nash plays with another kid, Nixon throws a fit," I sighed.

"They've got that brother bond. There's nothing wrong with it. My brothers and I had it," he said to me.

Then the next thing I knew is I felt a gush.

"Um, Betty Crocker, if you needed to use the bathroom, why didn't you tell me?"

"Well, grease monkey because my water broke!"

"Now? You're not due for another month!"

"The twins have other plans!"

I did not understand why we were yelling at each other, but we were. Nate got up and helped me up. I had to change my clothes three times. Then he helped me to the car. As he was getting ready to pull out, I said, "Nate!"

"What?" Nate yelled.

"Where's Nash and Nixon?"

"Shit."

He got out of the car, ran into the house, grabbed both boys, and hurried back to the car with them. He got them in their car seats and drove to the hospital. Don't judge. When you're in labor, you're not thinking about anything but pain.

As they took me back, Nate called Jonas to come to stay with the boys. Yeah, this wouldn't sit well with Lucille. Never call a sibling over a grandmother, especially if the grandmother is Lucille.

It didn't take long for the boys to enter the world. Nathan arrived first, followed by Noah, two minutes later. Both were healthy. I guess when you're pregnant with twins, you don't make it to your due date. That didn't surprise me, considering none of my boys made it to their due date.

After this, I do not want any more kids. Four were enough.

Once they cleaned me up and got me settled, everyone came to visit. Lucille gave Nate an earful, and I knew she would. Nash and Nixon looked at their baby brothers with awe.

The best part is they looked similar but not identical, which made us tell them apart. Thank God.

I looked at my family. Four boys in three years was a lot to handle. On the plus side, I'm almost finished with school.

Nate and I made an incredible team, and I couldn't have asked for a better partner.

CHAPTER 39

NEW NEIGHBORS

Nate was getting Nash and Nixon dressed, and I took care of the twins when we heard a truck. The new neighbors must move in.

He came in after getting the older boys situated and helped me with the twins. I picked up Nathan, and he picked up Noah. Being the nosy people we were, we checked them out. I mean, you always want to know who your neighbors are, right? Make sure they aren't some serial killers.

We walked outside and saw movers taking things into the house, but we didn't see the homeowners. Nate walked over to a mover. "Excuse me. Are the owners around?"

"No, sir," the mover answered.

"But you're moving items in?"

"Yes, sir," the mover replied.

"Um, okay," he said as he turned and walked back over to me.

"Well," I say to him.

"Owners aren't here," he shrugged.

I looked at him. That was odd. You would think most homeowners would want to be there with the movers. Great, we have weirdos moving in next to us.

I was putting the twins down for a nap when I heard crying. What are those boys getting into now? I walked out of the room and went downstairs to the kitchen. Thank God Nate had two ways of getting downstairs.

I opened the back door to see Nash helping a junior girl up who was crying.

"Nixon! That's not nice," Nash told him.

"I don't like her, Nash! She's yucky!" Nixon said with a face.

Great, my five years old and three years old were arguing.

"She's not yucky!"

I walked out, "Boys! What's going on out here?"

"Nix pushed her down," Nash said, pointing to the junior girl who was rubbing her eye and jutting out her bottom lip.

"Mommy, I don't like her!"

I watched her lip quiver and walked over to her. I knelt and looked at her, then noticed the scrape.

"Do you have a boo-boo?"

She nodded. "Okay. Let's go take care of your boo-boo," I whispered to her, standing up and holding out my hand. She reached up and grasped my hand with her little hand. I looked at Nixon. "We'll talk about being nice later."

I walked her into the kitchen and picked her up, setting her on the counter. I pulled out a first aid kit from under the sink and cleaned up her scrape; then I put a Scooby doo bandaid over it.

"How old are you, sweetheart?"

She held up two fingers.

"What's your name?"

"Maggie," she said in a tiny voice.

"Where do you live, Maggie?"

She pointed to the house next door.

"So, you're our new neighbor," I said with a smile. She stared at me with these big blue eyes, and she had ringlet curls. She was adorable.

I heard the door open and close. "Pat, I'm home!"

"I'm in the kitchen!"

He walked in and stopped. "When did we have another kid, and was I awake when it happened?"

"We didn't, and this one isn't ours. It's the new neighbor's kid." I rolled my eyes at him.

He walked over to her and looked at her. "Well, sweetheart, what is your name?"

"Maggie," she squeaked. He smiled at her and said, "Well, Maggie, let's get you home before your parents worry." He lifted her off the counter and set her down. Then he held out his hand, and she took it. She looked up at him and smiled. Oh dear, Maggie has a crush on Nate.

Nate walked Maggie back next door and opened it, only to get a surprise of his own.

"Brian?" Nate exclaimed.

"Nate?" Brian responded.

"You're our new neighbor," he asked him, shocked.

"Apparently," Brian looked down to see Maggie standing there, holding Nate's hand. He turned and yelled, "Tricia, Maggie got out again!"

"Well, you're watching her! I have a nail appointment!"

Nate looked at him as he turned back around. "So, you and Tricia got married?"

"Only because she got pregnant," he scoffed.

"I see."

"I'll take her," he said, taking Maggie's hand from him. He picked her up and set her down inside the house.

"You know, any time you want us to watch her, we'd be more than happy. I mean, we got four of our own," Nate mentioned to him.

"Yeah, I'll keep that in mind. Thanks for bringing Maggie home."

"Yeah, sure," Nate spoke through gritted teeth.

Then Maggie slipped past Brian and toddled over to Nate. She tugged at his pant leg. Nate looked down and then crouched down. "Yes, Maggie?"

"Hug." She held out her arms to him. Nate couldn't resist and hug her. Then he let go of her as Brian walked up, picked her up, carried her into the house, and closed the door.

Nate walked back to the house and inside. I was getting dinner situated and had the boys already at the table. He walked over to me. "Well, did you return, Maggie?"

"Yeah, but you never believe who her parents are."

"Who?"

"Brian and Tricia Holloway," he grumbled.

I did a double-take, "What?"

"Yeah, and I've got to be honest. There wasn't a lot of warmth between them and her. It was like she was more of an inconvenience than their child. Tricia worried about her nail appointment, and Brian seemed bothered."

"That poor girl," I said, worry filling my voice.

"I told him if he ever needed us to take her, we would be more than happy to," he said to me.

"It would give the boys someone to play with, and it would be nice to have a junior girl around," I smiled.

"Why, Mrs. Gray, are you telling me you would like another?" I gave him a look, and he said, "Okay, I'm checking." He raised his hands in defense.

My husband has lost his damn mind.

CHAPTER 40

NO MORE!

Scratch that. I know my husband lost his damn mind after finding out I was pregnant once again. I didn't understand. I was on birth control and took it.

The twins were almost two, so; I figured we finished. We weren't. The doctor confirmed it, and boy, did I have questions. Birth control is ineffective when you're on antibiotics.

I was not a happy camper when I got home.

"How?" He yelled.

"Because someone upstairs thinks this is hilarious," I spat.

"Why are you getting mad at me?"

"Because I told you I was not feeling good, that's why I was on antibiotics," I spoke.

"Wait a minute; you jumped me. Remember?"

I looked at him and thought about it; then I remembered what happened that night. "Oh, yeah," well shit.

"Oh yeah," he mocked me.

I gave him a look and said, "You are getting snipped. Make an appointment."

He gave me a look as I turned and said, "Are you coming or what?"

"Where are we going?" He questioned me.

"To the bedroom, duh," I rolled my eyes at him.

Who argues with that logic? All I can say is that this pregnancy was different. I was amorous, and Nate loved every minute.

He also got snipped. Five kids were plenty, plus Maggie was over even though the boys and she fought like cats and dogs except Nash. He took a shine to her.

Baby Nolan arrived, and when deciding his name, we picked it at random. I love babies, but I'm finished having them. By the age of twenty-five, I had five kids. Five was plenty.

There was a knock at the door, and I opened it to see a junior girl with brown curls and blue eyes standing there.

"Hi Pat," she grinned.

"Hi, Maggie," I smiled.

"Do you like my dress?" She twirled around in it.

"It's beautiful," I complimented her.

"Thank you. Mommy bought it for me because she is going out of town with Daddy," she said.

"Oh, well, would you like to stay here for a few days while they're gone?"

"I can't. Mommy said I already have a babysitter," she frowned.

Nate walked in and saw us. "Maggie, is that a fresh dress?"

"Yes, it is! Do you like it, Nate?"

"Yes, I do. It's beautiful," Nate complimented Maggie as he crouched in front of her. "Maggie, would you like some ice cream?"

Her face lit up. "Really?"

"Sure, Pat and I were going to have a bowl, aren't we?" he asked, looking at me.

"Sure, we can. A scoop of ice cream won't hurt," I said, getting out the ice cream and pulling down dishes. I dropped a scoop in eight bowls, and Nate called the boys down. I placed them on the table, and each boy took a seat while Nate placed Maggie on the counter.

"Why does she get to sit up there?" Nixon asked.

"Because all girls are princesses and treated that way," Nate reminded him.

"Is Mom a Princess?" Nathan asked him.

He looked at me. "Nope, she is my queen."

"Do princesses always wear pretty dresses?" Nash asked.

"The special one does. Boys, we should treat girls like princesses. They should have a pretty dress and should never cry," Nate said to them, and they all stared at him. Nolan was too busy with his ice cream to notice.

"Well, is Maggie a princess?" Nash asked him.

"I'm not sure why?"

"Because she is wearing a pretty dress," he said with those steel-grey eyes he had. The same color Nate had, and I knew that look. Nate had the same look for me, oh, boy.

Life with Nate and the boys was incredible. We had our difficulties, but we were the best team out there. With a girl living next door, it made things even more interesting for all of us.

I can see why Lucille so endured with me. When you have a house full of boys, you need girl time, and with Maggie, I got it.

Brian and Tricia were always going away, so I spent time with her, as did Nate.

We wanted her to have some kind of family and parental figures that she lacks at home. What happened next would change even everything?

CHAPTER 41

TIME JUMP: WE'RE GOING TO HAVE COMPANY

It had been twelve years of chaotic craziness, but I wouldn't change it for the world. The boys grew up. Nash is twenty, Nixon is eighteen and a senior. Nathan and Noah are seventeen and junior, while Nolan is fifteen and a freshman. One down, four to go, trying to get them through high school.

Maggie was around a lot more, and going to school with the boys was a genuine treat. I don't know why they felt the need to give the poor girl a hard time. She was such a sweetheart.

Nash went through Europe for a year. He left last year. After his breakup with Sarah, he felt the need to spread his wings. That left us with the four younger boys at home.

Until Nate got a phone call from Brian one day. Let's say this would affect us.

"So, let me get this straight. You both decided you needed a year-long vacation because you're stressed?" Maggie said to her parents as they stood in front of her.

"Ah, yes," Brian said.

"But you don't have jobs. You live off of mom's inheritance," she said as a matter of fact to them.

"But raising kids is stressful," Tricia said.

Maggie stood up. "You have one. Pat and Nate have five and work full time, with Pat even earning a degree. If we should stress anyone, it should be them!" She yelled at both of them.

"See it from our perspective, Maggie. Parents need a break," Brian said to her in a snooty tone.

"So, why you're away gallivanting around, doing God knows what, where will I be staying?"

"That's the best part. You stay with Nate and Pat," he said.

"What? Oh, hell, no! I hate their sons, and they hate me! And you want me to stay with them?"

"Yes," her parents answered.

"No!"

"Well, too bad. We have already decided on it. For seventeen years, I had to forgo a lot for you. Now I want to have some fun," Tricia said to her, looking at her nails.

"Forgo a lot for me? You haven't even been around for me. You leave me with babysitters, or Pat looks after me," she said.

"Oh, stop being a spoiled brat and go pack," Tricia ordered her.

"I hate you both," Maggie grumbled as she stormed up the stairs to pack.

"Finally," Brian said.

"Well, it won't matter because once we're gone, she is their problem and not ours," Tricia said as she walked away.

Some things never change.

Nate and I gathered the boys together to tell them about Maggie. They were less than receptive to it.

"No way!" Nixon exclaimed.

"Come on, Dad! We don't even like her," Nathan yelled.

"Too bad! She's coming to stay," Nate declared.

"But why?" Noah whined.

"Because her parents asked us, and we accepted," I told them.

"This is such horseshit," Nixon yelled.

"Language," I yelled at him.

"Look, I don't know what beef you boys and Maggie have with each other. You better work it out because she's staying here for a year," Nate said.

"A year? Man," they groaned.

That went better than expected. The doorbell rang, and Nate looked at the boys, "Behave."

They all looked at each other, and he answered the door. There stood Brian, Tricia, and Maggie.

"Thanks again for doing this, Nate," Brian said in phoniness. God, I hate him. He was still the same asshole from high school.

"Yeah, sure," Nate said through gritted teeth.

"Well, we are off. Bye now," Brian said as they left. They didn't even give Maggie a hug or kiss. What was that?

"I'm out of here," Nixon said, storming past us and out the door.

I looked at Maggie. "Nixon is cranky."

"Whatever, is there someplace I can set my stuff?" She asked, her tone icy.

"Yeah, sure, come on, I'll show you Nash's room," Nate said, grabbing her bags and taking them upstairs. She followed him, and something happened. That wasn't the Maggie I know.

"Well, we're going to our rooms," Nathan said as Noah followed Nathan.

"Boys?" I said, getting their attention.

"Yeah, ma?"

"Behave," I said to both of them with a look.

"Pft, yeah, okay," Nathan laughed. Oh, boy.

I turned and saw Nolan sitting there. I walked over. "Hun, you've been quiet. Is everything okay?"

He stood up and looked at me. "Ma, there is a desirable girl here who is not my mother. Everything is perfect," he smirked. He walked by me as I tried to say something, oh good god.

Nate came downstairs a few minutes later.

"Is Maggie all settled?" I asked him.

"Yeah, and she's not thrilled. She said two words to me," Nate said to me.

"I'm sure she's fine," I said to him.

"I hope so because I have a feeling the boys give her a run for her money," he said.

"Oh, I don't think it's the boys so much as it's her. I learned from growing up with you and your brothers is it takes a special girl to hold her own with the Gray boys."

"Wait, but we ended up together," he said to me.

"Yeah, but if you remember, it didn't start that way. We didn't like each other," I reminded him as I walked away.

He thought about it and then said, "You're kidding, right? Pat? Patty? Betty Crocker!"

He followed me. It would be an exciting year.

CHAPTER 42

HERE COMES THE GRAY BROTHERS

Adjusting to having a girl in the house was interesting. Having a seventeen-year-old girl in the house was even crazier. They fought, fought, and fought.

It started with the twins. They decided they wanted to have a little fun. So, they felt the need to decorate our front yard with her underwear.

Nate and I pulled up from shopping to see bras and panties strewn everywhere. Then we heard yelling, "I'll kill you demon spawn from hell!"

"We leave them alone for one day, and this happens," Nate sighed.

"Come on, let's get this cleaned up," I said to him as I got out of the car. We picked up all her underwear and brought them inside.

"Nathan and Noah," Nate yelled.

"Yeah, Dad?"

"Get your asses down here now!"

They came jogging down the stairs as Nate held up Maggie's underwear in his hand.

"This is what you're doing. I take it?"

"Sometimes, you have to make the yard pretty with lace," Nathan smirked, causing Noah to snicker.

"Go get the groceries, then you're both grounded," Nate said to them.

"What?" They all exclaimed.

"You heard your father," I told them. They walked by us, grumbling. I took Maggie's things from him and went to the washer so that I could clean them. So it starts.

Maggie got even with the twins and put itching powder in all their underwear. They didn't realize something could be wrong until breakfast when they itched.

"What are you boys doing?" Nate asked them.

"Nothing," they both said.

"Then quit itching your junk at the table," he ordered them.

A few minutes later, they itched again.

"Nathan and Noah," Nate said to them.

"Dad, we can't help it. We have to itch," Noah said, itching even harder.

"I guess then you should know I put itching powder in your underwear," Maggie said. She held up a bottle of itching powder. "Gives a whole new meaning to the word jock itch, doesn't it?"

They both glared at her as they got up and ran upstairs, slamming the door behind them.

I looked at Nate, and he looked at me, and we tried not to laugh. But they deserved it for what they did.

For two weeks, Nixon wasn't home much. We hardly saw him until I caught him one night coming in.

"Nixon?"

He stopped and turned to me. "What?"

"Don't use that tone with me, young man," I scolded.

"Sorry, ma," Nixon replied to me.

"What's going on, honey?"

"Nothing," Nixon answered.

"Nixon, talk to me," I said to him. He was always so hard to read. He would tell us if he was unhappy, but it seemed ever since Nash left, he's been even unhappier.

"I miss Nash," he said to me.

"Nix, we all miss Nash," I said to him.

"But you don't understand. Nash's my best friend, and he's gone. I have no one to talk to," he told me.

"You have your father and me along with your brothers," I reassured him.

"It's not the same. You wouldn't understand," Nixon said as he turned and walked away. I may not understand, but I know someone that would.

I walked into the bedroom, and Nate was sitting in bed, reading.

"I see Nixon is home," he said to me.

"Yeah," I said, letting out a sigh. I sat down on the bed and looked at Nate. "Nate, you can explain something to me."

He set his book down and looked at me. "I can try."

"Nixon said I wouldn't understand about him missing Nash. What did he mean?"

"He means that Nash is his best friend and brother. Nash is the only one that gets Nixon."

"What do you mean?"

"Nash is the big brother. He has a calming effect on Nixon. Nash takes charge and handles everything. With him not being here, Nixon feels like he has to be in charge. It's the alpha mentality. Nixon isn't an alpha-type personality," Nate explained to me.

"I miss Nash," I said to him.

"I do too, but you and I both know if he didn't go, we would lose him," he reassured me. "Baby, he'll be home before you know it."

Nate pulled me to him. I couldn't wait to see Nash when he came home, but I also knew it would be crazy when he returned to find Maggie here. He didn't know about her staying here, and with him gone, I didn't think it would matter.

I had a feeling it would matter more than anyone realized.

I folded clothes and placed them in a basket to take upstairs. As I stepped onto the top step, I heard Maggie yell, "Nolan, give me back my bra, you little brat!"

As Nolan ran down the hallway, waving her bra around like it was a flag.

"Nolan, stop taking Maggie's underwear," I said. I snatched the bra from him and tossing it to her as she passed him in the hallway.

"Aww, ma, you're no fun," he whined.

"Well, when you have kids of your own, then you can be no fun." I shrugged as I walked away. He walked away, and I winked at Maggie before she returned to her room.

I walked into our room and set the basket down on the bed.

Life as a Gray has been exciting. What started as neighbors for us ended up with one hell of a story. As I look back to how it all started, I wondered if I would do things differently. Then I realized, no. I wouldn't because everything turned out perfectly imperfect, and I wouldn't have it any other way.

*To continue with **The Gray Brothers.***

Made in the USA
Columbia, SC
10 December 2020